DAYTON'S ISLAND

Felicia Saltzman

Dedicated to my husband, Lucas—the hero in my own story. Thank you for your endless love and support.

Chapter 1 *A Most Unfortunate Beginning*

Dayton

My muscles tense under the weight of my Sig Sauer, though I hold it with the familiarity a product of the streets would be expected to.

Fog fills every crevice and shadow. Like walking through cream, I wade deeper into the alley and hear only the hitching of my breath. I step on a Heineken bottle, green glass tinkling. I stiffen, tightening my grip on the gun. I stop breathing to listen.

My lungs burn and I think I'm tempting fate. I try to focus past the buzzing in my ears.

You do this for me kid and it's the last thing you'll need. No more scraping or begging. You'll be a Condor. And once you're a Condor, we look out for own.

No one ever looked out for me. Never enjoyed the warmth of a home or the simplicity of eating a meal with family. Family—the word rolls around in my mind. But not long enough to be distracting . . . or make mistakes. Though there is a more violent voice in my head becoming louder by the second. It lingers, like warm brandy on the tongue, in the most enticing way.

This is suicide. They have sent you to your death.

I am jerked from my fear by the voices of two men—French, and amiable with one another. My time for thinking is over. It is now or never.

At the alley entrance, I press my shoulder blades against the bricks and clutch the gun tighter. The roar of blood in my ears dulls their voices. But I need to hear them. I need to know if Zachariah is here. I was told he would be.

Molin said I only have this one job. This one last time and then it's over. Will it ever be over?

"Do they really taste better?"

"These?" A chuckle—smoky in the night. "Indeed. I cannot bear to ever part with them. A favorite since my youth. I've been warned to quit."

"What is the point of living, unless we live a little, eh?"

The flow of conversation is lazy. Comfortable. And exactly the sort of space I plan to interrupt. My greatest chance for success will be in speed and accuracy, which I happen to be known for. Thank God.

In the slush of fog, the anticipation reaches a pinnacle. I've never taken a man's life like this. Thought about it, yes, many times and I have seen the result of my defense with a death. One cannot live in Amsterdam without getting caught between a brick wall and a knife at some point. To fight, is to live. But to stand on this precipice, to be certain of where the bullet will go and how it will kill. I didn't think I could. Until now.

The seconds between my decision to move into the open and that of desertion seem like years. But without a command, I step out, swing my firing arm in the direction of the voices as I stride into view.

Their heads snap toward me. The men seem surprised by my appearance, and my weapon—but it seems no one is in a hurry to run. Pointing it directly at the one I can only assume is Zachariah, I am numb.

I've never seen the man in person. I have only his photo. Eyes like soft skies and a long thin oiled mustache mark him my target. The other man—of equal height, but a rangier and athletic build—stares with open shock.

"He's just a kid."

"I'm not a kid," I say, through gritted teeth. My jaw is tight. My finger is locked on the trigger.

"No." Zachariah shakes his head. "He's not. Not with that pretty gun in his hands. A Sig. That is what you've brought, isn't it?"

I focus the barrel at his chest. "Is your name Zachariah?"

He settles his hands into his pockets. His calm irritates me. "That would make things easier for you, wouldn't it? If I identify myself so you bring back assurances of a job well done."

"Your name."

Skinny man lifts his chin at me. "He won't do it— kid is near shitting himself."

"I'm not a kid." I struggle for control of my voice. "I'm nineteen." It's not too far from the truth. I want to get this done, get it over with now. But instead of squeezing the trigger, I stall. "I need your name. Or I'll shoot both of you to be sure."

"Do you know what you risk by threatening me?" Zachariah speaks to me in slow, careful tones. "What will happen to you when you do this?"

At least I am comforted he's worried I might actually shoot.

"Yes."

Skinny makes a snorting noise, then, in a move faster than I can follow, produces a gun and points it at me.

I made a perilous mistake. I won't live past these moments.

"Game over, kiddo."

I smirk, forcing vomit back. "I've got a shot at your

boss. Even if you shoot me, I can get Zachariah."

"Brave."

Zachariah smiles. "Put the gun down, Jacque. He's not going to shoot me."

"So sure, are you?" I ask, as my hands tremble. My shirt clings to me like a second skin. Where determination roosted only a half hour previous, terror now sits.

"*Oui.* But let's find out, shall we?"

He steps closer, standing in front of me, the picture of amusement as my gun shakes. I adjust, but my arms are stiff and my fingers near-locked to stone.

"Will you shoot me then?"

For the first time, I detect a threat.

The white dress shirt exposes a suntan. I rest the gun at the top of the crucifix on his heavy gold chain.

"I . . . I'm not sure. What will you give me not to?"

Zachariah laughs. "*Mon Dieu*, I like you little one. Ferocious. Let's see." He glances back to Jacque. "You can work for me."

"Leave the Condors? Become a traitor?"

"Well." He examines me, ignoring the weight of the barrel. "Yes, yes that would be needed. I have just the position for a young man like yourself, who has enough fire and promise to whet the appetite."

I can't believe I am considering his offer as a possibility. I should have pulled the trigger when he was at the wharf with his expensive black cigarettes and favorite goon. But it's too late. I'll be killed now. I'll die.

"You'll kill me the moment I drop this gun . . . I would."

"Then it is fortunate I am not you, *oui*?"

His voice is strangely gentle—paternal. It could be a trap, but I let my gun slide downward to my side.

I stare, daring him to have Jacque kill me now, but I already know he won't. It's why I lowered my Sig, and stand vulnerable in front of one of the most successful mercenary leaders in France—since before I was born. I may have been raised in the gutters, but I know criminal royalty when I see it. I know his stories.

"There, there." Zachariah slings an arm over my shoulders. "You are going to be my new best friend. I've been needing fresh blood. And most certainly a new perspective on the Condors. Don't you think, Jacque?"

He shrugs. But his eyes do not agree.

"What's your name then, kid?"

"My name?" It feels like I'm stuck in cement—I can't think past the mist rolling in. It's like the horror film, The Fog. I expect a fantastical skull ship to sail into the wharf at any second.

"*Oui, oui,* we must call you something."

I'm wondering if I've fallen asleep in my bunk with a bottle of whiskey. I'll wake up soon and Molin will come hollering down the pipes for me to get my ass over to him.

"Dayton." I hesitate as a giant white yacht comes into view, piercing the gray with her elegant bow. "Jepsen."

She's massive, something I've only heard stories of. The yacht pulls alongside. She's at least three stories.

Zachariah waits for Jacque to step around him to board.

"Well, Dayton Jepsen, I hereby welcome you to the ranks of the Phantoms. And as you can see, we are many." He indicates the men scrambling to ready the yacht for boarding.

I experience something entirely foreign—excitement, and then fear.

Twelve years later . . .

"I've told you time and time again, I'm fine. I don't need company. Nor do I want it. I need some time off, Zach."

I wait for his usual diatribe. His warm laughter suits our conversation.

In the twelve years since I boarded his ship and joined the Phantoms, I have become more of a son than a leading commander in this small army of mercenaries. Having recently celebrated his fiftieth birthday, Zachariah is often concerned over my welfare and health, rather than my kill margins. My numbers are impeccable.

Having a fretting father is something both of us are learning. I don't take it for granted.

"Dayton, I wouldn't ask if I wasn't worried. You have not been yourself these last weeks. The men noticed."

"You've had Jacque spying on me."

"He is mine to do with as I please, as are you."

I pinch the bridge of my nose to quell a budding headache and look to where blue waters and white sand wait for me. "I'm tired Zach. I need a break. Give me a few weeks to recharge and then we'll—" I breathe in the salty air, wondering how on earth I could ever consider going back. How I could consider not. "We'll talk."

"Yes." Zach sounds exhausted over the phone. "It's what I'm afraid of. Stay in touch. I'm in the area if you need me and as always, take care of yourself."

"Wouldn't want to lose your best asset."

Zach snorts, but it's with an affection I've grown to expect. "You know it's more than that. Try not to get lost on that little island of yours."

I hang up, in the open sweep of kitchen, I lean on the granite countertop. The contrast of cool stone to balmy air brings me a measure of peace I rarely have when the day is done—and it is simply me . . . alone. I've been on my private island in the Dominican Republic for about twenty hours and already, the tension is lifting. I sense the subtle change of warrior to man. It makes me . . . unsure. As if I shut off entirely, I risk an attack. I don't like the sensation.

I'm on the balcony looking at the glistening water of the infinity pool on the walk-out deck. With a dug-in basement, the main floor and upper, the beach house is not just roomy, it's my palace.

Six years ago, I amassed enough fortune to purchase about anything a man could desire. I spent every penny on this island. On building this house. Zach called it my 'fortress of solitude' and laughed it off as a needed outlet. What I didn't tell him, was that I see myself here and only here, until age catches up with me. Now, with my bank accounts bursting, my kill ratios higher than any in the history of the Phantoms, I am tired.

I do need time . . . to decide. Zach must understand this, or he wouldn't have told me to take my allotted weeks off at the island. Deep within, where the souls go to haunt me, I know my time for killing is over. I'm finished.

I stare into the seascape and wonder about my life choices and my future, then head back into the kitchen for a beer. There is plenty of time for thinking later. After I swim in the pool, and maybe down a few more beers.

The air is so thick tonight I am far from sleep, skin peppered in sweat, with my back to the gauzy curtains drifting in the breeze. They feather over the hardwood floor, then settle back like mice scurrying, I am awake so long, the shapes in the room blur, then form into men. Ugly and odd-shaped, but enemies nonetheless and I squint to force them back into their places . . . back into my chairs and plant stands.

I'm distracted until the back door creaks open . . . an intruder. I get up, neglecting shirt or pants, remaining in my briefs. I pull my Glock from under the bed. I switch so easily back into who I've become these last years.

The feet softly pad through the back entryway over the concrete to the open living and kitchen space. I can sense their movement as easily as if I were steering them with my mind. I wait until the feet are at the window where I was earlier. But this person is not welcome here, and I don't play well with others. Mentally, I've already killed him and thinking of the best location to dispose the body. A frightening aptitude, however survivalist.

When I reach the bottom of the stairs, I stare at the silhouette of a woman in front of the French doors.

Barefoot, wearing a long white linen dress, her trim body outlined by moonlight. And she's angelic. Fragile as a blossom. Her hair streams like water down her back in a shade too difficult to distinguish in the shadows. It beckons to be touched.

I am caught like a trapped animal at the picture she portrays. Disgusted, I clench my jaw and shred the image internally. She's a target. An intruder. Emotions are the heart of mistakes, and mistakes have no place in my line of work.

Chapter 2 *Well, Hello There…*

Esme

I'm here. Finally here.

The sea raging against the rocks contrasts with the soft honeysuckle breeze I suspect is unique to the island. And I revel in it, lean into it, with hands open as if to pull the environment into my soul.

I thought I'd never get here.

Flights, phone calls, and the final leg of the journey—I begged the dock master to allow me private boarding to this masterpiece of an island. The headaches have been worth it. I need this. Oh, how I need this.

Tears of relief and sorrow blur my vision. A breath of fresh air grounds me, as I hug my arms to my middle.

"Hands up, lady."

Turning away from the window, I reach for the blade between my breasts. When I stop, a man, long and lean, has a black gun pointing at my face.

"Who sent you?"

"Sent me?" My hands are shaking, though I have a solid grip on the blade, but it will do little good with a bullet between my eyes.

"Don't play stupid, honey. This is a private island. You didn't accidently walk into my house."

My fingers tighten on the blade. "I know it's a

private island. But it can't be yours."

"Is that so?"

His voice is strangely gentle. I resist the urge to run. Maybe it's the long days of travel, or the weariness of months without a proper place to sleep, and no guarantee of a meal. I'm not sure, but I square my shoulders and meet his challenge.

"Yes! It is so! I've been personally invited by the man who owns this island. You, are in the wrong, sir. I demand to know why are you are here!" A blush warms my cheeks when his gaze is on my face. "And, may I ask why you are still pointing that gun at me?"

"You are armed as well, mademoiselle."

I am shocked the man speaks any French at all with his Dutch accent. And can he make a good argument when I peg him as a thief? Perhaps another islander who wants to steal my father's house in his absence . . . a squatter.

My father. I don't know if I'll ever get used to hearing that . . . claiming another person as my own.

"This knife is hardly comparable to a gun."

"Perhaps."

"Listen." I reign in my temper. To show him the knife then lower it to my side. "I don't want to hurt you. And you don't want to hurt me. Yes? Let's talk like adults. Like two friendly people with a little misunderstanding."

"There is no misunderstanding. You are standing in my home . . . that I built, on my island. The deed to this house and the island has been in my name for six years. You should have done your homework, better than to try bullshitting your way into here."

There is a ring of truth to his voice. And a quiet threat.

"Then call the police. I'm sure they'll sort things out."

"There are no police out here. If there were, they would not come quickly if I called. I have a certain reputation for liking my peace and privacy."

I am alert. I can't help the need to defend myself. To fight back. My months of freedom have renewed my sense of self and pride I thought were destroyed. I would celebrate my ability to stand up to a man, especially this one, but he hasn't lowered his gun. Either way, I've been raised to fight for what I want and it appears—I might die doing it.

"We can be reasonable."

"Yes, we could. What is your name?"

I'm surprised. There's a shift in conversation, yet he keeps the gun aimed at my head. I'm sweating through my sundress. "Put the damn gun down, and I'll answer you."

"Answer me first. And I might consider it."

He's a stubborn pig.

"Esme."

"Esme. Italian?"

"Sure. Maybe. You going to put the gun down?"

"Your last name."

I grit my teeth. Angry at him, and my father. I should have known it was too good to be true. A liar. Just like everyone else.

"Costello. You happy?"

"Latin origin. Irish?"

"American actually. Why the hell do you care?"

The gun lowers and my breathing slows. But there is the minor complication of being trapped on an island at midnight with a stranger.

"I'm trying to understand why you're here, Ms. Costello. And I'm finding it difficult with your attitude."

"My attitude? Listen, I didn't ask to be put in this position. There is a misunderstanding! I was sent here. I was given keys. Which work by the way, or I wouldn't be standing in your living room. Maybe you need to be careful who you give keys to."

He pauses. I hope he might be considering my

honesty. I try to restrain tears as he brings up the lights in a blinding display. Staggering back a few steps, I grope for the counter for support. I'm sure as hell glad I can grab it, because the man looks like he slithered off the cover of a GQ magazine.

Or a rough and tumble version of it.

Six foot something, he towers over me and is intimidating from across the room. His collar length hair is sun-streaked dirty blonde. He's bare, except for black briefs . . . and bronzed, and Mediterranean, at least in part. He's like an Apollo . . . only this Apollo has a gun and is glaring at me with green eyes.

"Dear God."

"Not what you expected?"

I'm not certain if I should blush, or be outraged. There is an armed half-naked man in a vacation house gifted as a place to hide.

"I don't know. Maybe. What . . . I mean—" I look away from him and out to the sea. "What I mean to say is, I was sent here. Given a key. And there has been a mistake. We should stick to solving this problem."

"Clearly."

I curtail swear words, and work to give him my best flight attendant smile. "Things got a bit heated for a second, and I lost my manners. But I'd like to start over. My name is Esme Costello. You have a lovely home." If . . . it is in fact yours.

There is a flicker of humor as he looks at me. He thinks me amusing. "My name is Dayton. Who told you the location and gave you a key?"

"I . . . my father did. I believe I mentioned that earlier."

"Yes. But you neglected to tell me his name. As you have a key to my home, I must say, I need the name."

"You're obviously the kind of man used to getting his way. But I am not comfortable giving you his name when you freely walk about carrying guns."

Dayton's eyes narrow. "I am used to it."

"I've known men like you before. Far too many."

Men like Carl.

"Mademoiselle, I doubt you have known any man like me. Now please, I don't want this to become . . . ugly, give me the name and I'll be happy to call them to come and pick you up."

"There is no one to pick me up. I was dropped off here." Tears tighten the back of my throat. "I bribed the dock master with a bottle of champagne to allow me on the last boat. He did. And I'm here. Damned if I know why I did it." I grip my dress trying not to tremble . . . trying to keep the cracks from splitting the mask I've been wearing for forty-eight hours. "The man who sent me here—I don't know him very well. But he told me not to give his name. Said it wasn't safe to do so."

"I think you might want to make an exception to that."

There's a threat in Dayton's voice. But I'm tired. I'm standing in a stranger's living room in the middle of nowhere. I've not eaten in twelve hours and my feet feel bruised to the bone.

"My father sent me."

"Yes, you said that already."

A chuckle bubbles up but I control it. "Yes well, I'm tired. And like I said, I don't know the man well, even though he is my father." I hesitate—to look Dayton directly in the eyes to gauge his reaction.

"His name is Zachariah Moncleve."

Dayton

She doesn't look like him.

I don't react. The betrayal I feel in knowing Zach

sent an unknown person to a place I've worked so hard to keep secret is too sour a pill to swallow . . . especially in the middle of the night. I can do nothing but wait. And prepare for the worst.

"Do you have a way to contact him?"

"He gave me his number."

"Good." I'm weighing the .45 in my hand as Esme Costello watches me. She doesn't know what to make of me. In a matter of seconds, it seems she has assessed me as attractive and dangerous. She may appear weak and fragile, but I doubt that is what is beneath. There is a jagged edge about her that denotes an extra layer worn . . . from repeated abuse.

"You can call him in the morning. Until then, I can offer you the guest bedroom."

Her eyes glisten with unshed tears. She is schooling her emotions, but it is clear she is close to crumbling.

Esme blinks rapidly, scrubbing her hands on her face. "Who is Zachariah to you? How do you know him?"

My irritation with Zach is spiraling to a new level. "He is a friend."

"A friend . . ."

"Until tonight, I thought him to be a very good one. I've worked for him for many years."

"Strange for him to send me here."

"Please help yourself to any food or drink you might want. There is a bathroom in the guest bedroom and fresh towels are stocked by housekeeping."

She stares at me. If there were a part of me swayed by cream skin and soft blue eyes, I'd be melted to the core.

She is nothing like Zach.

Nothing at all.

Why the hell did he send her to me?

"Esme?"

Her eyes meet mine. There is strength behind the exhaustion. And it's . . . unsettling. Attractive.

"Lock your door and don't wander the house at night. I don't usually ask before shooting."

Ignoring her, I head upstairs. My door isn't thick enough to keep her presence out of my sleep.

Esme

I can hear him breathing over me. Smell the expensive brandy he likes. It's dripping onto my skin. It makes nausea roll in my gut and I curl into a ball even as I struggle to remain motionless.

If he thinks I'm sleeping, then he won't want as much from me.

He won't hurt me.

He'll just touch.

I breathe in evenly, wait for his messy mouth to stumble to mine—for him to attempt to rouse me with a drunken kiss. But it doesn't. I remain stiff and unmoving.

"Bitch."

The whisper makes my skin flush with goosebumps and I wait for seconds, minutes, hours until his grip on my arms lessens and he collapses at my side.

My breathing slowly returns to normal. My heart smooths its pace. And I sink deeper into the silk sheets I have grown accustomed to . . . and despise.

I awake abruptly and can smell the stale brandy in the air.

Light spills into the unfamiliar bedroom, and on the mattress. Damask crème bedding covers me like a dream. A dream within a dream. Or a dream clouding the nightmares.

My breathing is slowing on its own.

I am far from Amsterdam. Far from those mistakes.

Far from Carl.

It has been four months and if I focus on the future, time will march forward, I will move on. The dreams will diminish. At some point, even my heart will forget. At least, I pray it will.

The gossamer curtains are as elegant as the bedding. They signal warmth, sunlight, and a new day. I close my eyes and bring my thoughts to the present. Or rather, my current predicament.

Saved by a man I hardly know, only to be handed to a green-eyed giant with a gun.

It's laughable.

Almost.

Sighing, I sit up and work my feet into the slippers I unpacked. Oversized pale fluff swallows my feet. How I managed to do anything other than melt into a mess of tears and snot the night before is impressive— especially when I stand in front of the bathroom mirror.

My eyes are shadowed with fatigue. My coloring is bordering on sickly. These last days have not been kind to my waist either. I've likely gained five pounds in the last week. Probably from stress and crappy hotel food— criminal to my favorite pair of Gucci jeans.

I'll have to reinstitute my exercise regimen. And drink those grainy morning protein shakes Carl demanded I choke down.

I press my palms to my swollen eyes. If I think of Carl or his name, one more time, I will throw myself over the railing and into the sea. It's nothing less than I deserve.

I comb my hair into a ponytail and choose a sapphire blue dress that compliments my skin regardless how pale it gets. I've hidden in this room long enough. Dayton will wait. A man like him won't give up his house simply because he's friends with Zachariah Moncleve.

Like a mouse escaping from its hole, I tiptoe into the hallway, and I want to hide. But I'm ensnared by the smell of bacon and coffee. It pulls me in the direction of the kitchen.

Dayton is standing over the stove, in gray slacks and white dress shirt, thank goodness. There is only so much staring at the floor I can do. He appears to make note of my appearance. He doesn't address me, but continues cooking—like a man well-versed in a kitchen. He completes omelets, bacon, and delicious-looking muffins. He offers me a curt smile and a cup of coffee.

I don't think it polite to request the cream and sugar I usually require. I smile and drink deeply. Black is better than nothing.

"Thank you. It smells wonderful."

"I hope you like quail."

I take another sip. He places a plate in front of me and gestures to the deck. The French doors are open and the Parisian style chairs and table on the deck are set for two. We sit as if this scenario between us is usual. Although the tension is evident.

"Do you mean the eggs are quail?" I said, taking my seat.

Dayton nods. I swear I see warmth beneath the frigidity. He cuts into his omelet. I follow his lead and eat quietly. Which is easy. It's delicious. I try not to eat too quickly and remind myself of the jeans I love. I will never be able to purchase another pair of Gucci jeans. I'll have to relish the one pair I own, and give it the proper respect it deserves . . . by being able to wear them.

As we finish the meal, I gaze at the water. "It's beautiful here."

"Yes."

I push some spinach around. "I can call my father at any time."

"I already called him."

I drop the fork. Dayton is looking at me—the way he did last night. I don't know whether to be worried or surprised.

"And?"

"We spoke about the situation and . . . he updated me on what exactly he wants done."

"Is he sending someone to get me? Did he say what happened? Why he sent me here?"

Dayton's eyes appear to change to silver and I'm reminded of a handsome dragon pestered by its meal. He sighs, and stands. "No."

"No to which?"

"Do you always find yourself asking so many questions?"

"Do you always find yourself so rude to strangers?"

"We aren't strangers, Esme. You've slept in my home and ate breakfast with me. I think we can upgrade our relationship to acquaintance."

I clamp my mouth shut at his retort, and determine not to fall into old habits. I've done this before . . . with the man who will not be named because I have no wish to throw myself off the balcony into the sea. I'm through with being bullied, especially when all I'm asking for are simple answers.

"You don't know me and I don't know you. That makes us strangers. Let's get that settled. And as for my father, I'd like to know what he said."

For the first time, there's a fissure in Dayton's shell and what I see has me backing up. He's furious—with me or Zachariah, I don't care. To witness anger, is to be wary of receiving swift punishment.

"He said no. He isn't coming for you. No one is. You are my responsibility for the time being. And if you'd like to know anything on the matter, call him yourself."

"Wait . . . wait. Your responsibility?"

"Isn't that what I said?" Dayton's veins stand out on his neck.

"Yes but, it makes no sense. He wanted to get me

away. To give me . . . to give me some time away from everything—in a safe place."

"So, I have been informed." Dayton grips the railing.

"I don't understand."

"That makes two of us. It hardly makes a difference. I work for Zachariah Moncleve. And as such, I am going to be your caretaker until further notice."

Caretaker . . . babysitter . . . jailer.

"You mean I can't leave."

"No. You can't."

"What did he tell you?"

"Enough. I know you were on the run after you killed a man and had to leave Amsterdam. The details were not discussed, and I can only assume it is meant to protect your dignity. Moncleve believes I don't need to know."

I grab for something solid. The railing is warm from the sun. I don't know if I am angry or relieved. My emotions are shredded. The Esme who left America in search of adventure, is long gone. Or, she is buried so deeply I cannot find her any longer.

"Do you believe you need to know?" My voice is weaker than I want.

Dayton mirrors my posture at the railing,

"You've been dropped off on my doorstep like some lost puppy. Wouldn't you like to know the details before you are forced into accepting this?"

"So I'm a lost puppy to you."

"Are you lost Esme?"

My eyes are moist. "Yes. But I certainly didn't ask for your help."

"No. You asked your father. And I work for him."

"I didn't know what else to do. I couldn't keep running because I ran out of money. I don't expect you to understand desperation. Particularly when you live in this behemoth of a house. At the time, I could do nothing else but call him. Now . . ." I cast a scathing look at him. He is ruggedly handsome. "I'm wishing there was something else I could have done."

He looks at me as he might a child. "I don't play well with others."

"Clearly." I try to calm the anger beneath the surface.

I've been in worse situations. Far worse. But I cannot help thinking this is some sort of punishment for my crimes. I'd been desperate after that night. Scared and unsure of what to do, it took me only three weeks to wind up sleeping on park benches. I called Zachariah, using the number on the piece of paper he gave me two years ago, and I accepted his words of calming reassurance. I hadn't thought of anything else. I wasn't prepared. Especially for the possibility I could be abandoned on a God-forsaken island in the Caribbean.

"You live here, all alone?"

"Some of the time."

"The alone bit, or the living here?"

"I live here part time."

I grasp for calm. A little time, a little air, and I'll think of a solution that won't involve being trapped on this island with a man who can't stand my presence any more than I can his.

"Sounds lonely."

Dayton surprises me with a laugh. It's rich and warm, nothing like the coolness he's given me since I met him.

"I'm far from lonely. When I need company, the mainland has all a man can want. I like solitude. Perhaps you aren't acquainted with the notion."

"Shocking." The jealousy softens me. I never could be alone and enjoy it.

"And what do you do every day then?"

"Whatever pleases me."

"What exactly do you do for my father that allows you such freedom?" I gesture at the expanse of house, trying to hide my suspicion. "And . . . wealth? I'm thinking it's not exactly legal."

"It's not. But if your father hasn't told you what he does, then I can't tell you what I do for him. Another day, another battle. Today, I'll give you the rules of the house."

"Rules?" He makes an excellent jailer. A better term than babysitter—with that dangerous glint in his eyes. He's angry. And doing an impressive job at chaining it.

"Yes. You are in my home. My island actually. And I have rules."

"Okay, let's hear them."

"I like things clean. And I enjoy cooking. So I'll do all of the cooking and you'll be taking care of your own laundry and messes. I don't do maid service."

I try not to grin like an ornery child. I'm not very charitable this morning. Not even with Dayton's excellent breakfast warming my stomach.

"That's easy enough. I don't like cooking and I know how to use a washing machine. Anything else?"

"Yes. I have a personal gym, which you are welcome to use, except between six and eight a.m. and nine to ten at night. The pool, will be unavailable to you from ten to eleven at night. The second floor of this house is completely off-limits."

"Okay."

I like swimming in the morning. And as for using the weight room or athletic equipment, I'm fairly certain I can squeeze in some time when his royal highness is not making use of them.

The man appears to study me with an expression of patience, although he's flicking his fingers. If I'm getting under his skin, it's a happy accident.

"You are not to leave the island without escort.

Ever. The mainland will be of minimal consequence to you during your stay. As for socializing, I'm not here to entertain, I will feed and care for you. I enjoy my quiet and will continue to enjoy it, though your presence here will undoubtedly chafe, whether or not you get bored here. Any questions?"

"Yes." I can tell he can hardly wait to be rid of me, but I don't give him the satisfaction. "May I use your telephone? Or is there a time frame I am allowed to use that as well? Maybe a chart would be helpful. To make sure I don't cramp your style."

A twitch of his mouth is the only indication he is amused by my dig. Or I suppose it could mean he's irritated.

"You may use the phone at any time you wish. As long as it is to call your father—and your father only. I have been informed you have no family or friends to call. I won't be monitoring your calls in person, I do have the ability to do so. If need be."

The stark reminder of no family, no friends, leaves me raw. I nod, ready to be rid of Dayton. I got my pound of flesh and I want to sulk.

"Am I allowed to explore the island? Alone?"

"As long as you make me aware of your plans before leaving and set strict times for your return."

"Like a curfew?" There's acid in my tone. I can't make myself care.

"Yes."

To have someone—anyone—care for me, and my life. I hate that I've reached this level. I'm prepared to face plant on the floor and cry like a baby. Dayton's voice seems to soften, or maybe I just want it to. And then indulge myself in a huge pity party.

"One more thing . . . you have wine?"

He nods.

"And chocolate?"

This time the amusement is obvious.

"It's in the pantry, top shelf. Help yourself. The phone is on the counter by the fridge. Feel free to let your old man have a piece of your mind. Dayton gives me a full smile. "I know I did."

For six hours, I wallow in my room. Or rather, the guest room, as this is not to be my permanent station. Wherever the hell that might be in the future, I pray it is far from the Dominican Republic . . . and green eyes.

I consume too much chocolate. And as much wine.

I postpone my call to dearest daddy until after I've a good cry and some time to think—to plan.

This results in a sloppy list of pros and cons scribbled on strands toilet paper. I read the list at the top of the bullet points.

I can't leave the island or get rid of my appointed guardian/jailer. And thus, I must cohabitate with a man who, although irritating, is rather handsome. I can avoid him easily if I want. Dropping the paper on the bed, I drink the remainder of my wine. The more I sit in waves of misery and pity, the more I decide how to make the best of this ridiculous situation.

It's an opportunity to relax on an island in the Dominican Republic. Something I will never likely get to do again. Who has the money for vacations when surviving is of paramount importance? Ignoring the thought, I continue to mentally check off what I will be enjoying— and smiling at my prospects.

The water is Prussian blue. Coconut and fresh ripe bananas scent the air. Having never been anywhere so tropical and secluded, I could get lost in the foliage of the island simply exploring.

I dig my way out of the thick comforter.

I could lie naked on my beach towel and attempt a tan. Or at least a deeper cream color. I have to wear sunscreen or risk permanent maiming by radiation, but the sun will do wonders for my dower mood.

It can be like a vacation for me. A time of rest. Where I put Amsterdam and all that happened there behind me. I can try to erase, bit by bit, the places Carl hurt, the ways he destroyed who I was. I could try.

I pull back the curtains, and stare at the sea.

I will forget him. I will eradicate him. And I'm going to enjoy this bloody island if it kills me. Or I get killed by Dayton. Or I kill him. He would have it coming, no doubt.

With this optimism flooding me, I step into my red Calvin Klein bikini, like a teenager gushing for prom. It's noon. And the pool should be free for my use. And damn it, I'm going to use it.

Walking through the house, I allow myself to feel wealthy and safe again. Most of all, safe. The concrete cools my bare feet, and the breeze wafting over the decks is luxurious. I take the stairs to the lower floor and walk out to the sunny pool area. The water is as inviting as I hoped. I am relaxed from the zinfandel I pilfered out of the kitchen, and I welcome the cold rushing over my head as I dive into the deep end.

I push off from the gem-toned tiles on the bottom and begin with the breaststroke, and my mind hazes out the rest of the way. Now this—with the waffling of water in my ears and the sun warming my back—is the stuff of dreams.

Chapter 3 *Tanning Issues*

Dayton

She has been swimming for an hour. Her strokes are like an obnoxious little fly on my window. I spent most of this last hour shuffling papers and getting absolutely nothing done, I now regret giving her access to the pool at all. Particularly because the second I saw her in that tiny red bikini, my heart fell and I stumbled over my feet.

I'm a grown man . . . used to knowing his boundaries, to seeing the goals and to having control when the time calls for it. But that hasn't stopped me from glancing out my window to watch Esme.

Like a pale mermaid carving through cerulean waves, she tortures me without even trying. And I'm allowing it. It's appalling.

I slam my pencil on the desk, and glare at the architectural drawings I've been perfecting for a guest house. Though I prefer to be alone, I think this home has always needed a smaller, sedate cousin for guests to enjoy their privacy.

I like Zach. And his crankier version, Jacque. Like father and uncle, they have stayed with me several times on my island. The guest quarters is something I've been looking forward to working on.

The situation with Zach colors my design and my focus. It distracts me from my ability to remain objective with his beautiful, surly, and wounded daughter—whom I knew nothing about until last night.

Admittedly, I was angry when talking to him about it.

Hurt, betrayed . . . petty emotions, but they are there nonetheless.

He said, 'It was my only choice. You would have done the same.'

Drop a young woman off with a killer for safe keeping? No. I can't imagine doing the same. But Zach doesn't see this way of life as criminal or dangerous. He doesn't see his employees as killers nor does he consider me, his best assassin, as a risk.

He should.

His words ring in my head.

'I didn't think you'd accept this if I told you beforehand. She needs you. She needs us. Can you really send her away after knowing that?'

Asshole. He knew I couldn't. He knew I would be drawn to her weakness and obligated to protect her. His lack of care for his daughter, got him exactly what he wanted. And I shouldn't be surprise. What could I expect of a man who can maneuver a new hire from a young man about to kill him. Zach is always ruthless when he wants something. To the point of blood.

The splashing stops. My attention is immediately drawn back to the windows where the only thing separating me from her line of vision is a sheer curtain. It makes her appear ethereal.

I watch her. My body tense as I pull my tongue back into my mouth. Instead of going inside to get out of the heat, she stretches out on a chaise lounge, leaning back to expose every inch of her luscious skin to the sun, in that tiny excuse for a bathing suit.

Fool.

Knowing I shouldn't, I take the stairs to the lower floor where cobblestones open into an outdoor oasis with the pool at the center. Palms sway amid the jabbering of watercolor birds. I'd stop and admire the scene if I wasn't so livid. Any self-control I pride myself on these last hours just crumbled.

I walk toward Esme's draped form, and my voice snaps like a whip. "Do you intend to burn every inch of your body? Or are you just that stupid?"

Her eyes widen as she looks around. She seems to notice me . . . several feet away. I'm standing under an umbrella—one she is neglecting to use.

"Stupid? No. I'm wearing sunscreen."

"It's been an hour. And you've been swimming. With skin like yours, you're probably already burning."

She sits up and frowns. She's wearing a pair of shiny aviators and they are as fitting as her miniscule bikini. She screams Milan, wealth and uncomfortable class. I have money now. I didn't always. But I've never felt comfortable around those who wear it well.

"Am I now to assume you are going to play the role of my daddy as well as my personal security?"

"My job is to be concerned with your welfare. Giving yourself third-degree burns happens to fall into that category."

Esme makes a fist, but remains relaxed in the chair.

"I believe it's free reign at the pool, isn't it? I'll be done soon and then you can use it, if you'd like. You look like you could cool off. Loosen up."

My jaw tightens when she adjusts herself and lies back, the picture of relaxation. Her skin glistens.

"I'm not accustomed to losing, mademoiselle."

"Then get used to it."

She looks like a satisfied cat after scarfing the canary. I could warn her how close I am to losing it, but I don't think I'm ready for the loss of control. So, I don't. I don't question what madness comes over me. I simply walk over and pick her up.

Apparently too shocked to resist, she stares at me with mouth agape and her aviators slipping on her nose. But as we get closer to the house she fights.

"Put me down! Now!"

"No."

"My father will hear of this."

"Good!"

My face is inches from hers.

She squirms, kicking her legs. I sling her over my shoulder. Her red-clad ass is by my cheek and her fists are pounding my back. By the time we reach the main floor, I'm enjoying myself. All the tension from earlier leaves with laughter and I don't regret this decision . . . I ought to. Esme resorts to calling me names, some of which, I've never heard of. I can only assume them to be of the American language.

I dump her, a little roughly, onto the crème colored sofa in the sitting room and wait for her anger to reach boiling point.

And she certainly doesn't disappoint me.

"How dare you!"

Face red, hair half-dried and mussed, she walks straight up to me and gives her best attempt at a punch. It reaches the top of my chest. It's like running into a thin branch. Mildly annoying, but adorable. Our height difference is pitiful.

"Be careful now, Esme. I only put up with so much

before I'm forced to respond."

"I don't care. You have no right to haul me about. You have no right to tell me anything!"

"This is my home. You are under my care. I have every right."

Her eyes are murderous, which only makes my smile wider. This is what I need. A fight. A way to needle the object of my irritation into revealing as much as I feel. If I'm to be affected by her, then I can only hope she feels the same. Mutual irritation should be good for housemates.

"I will be calling my father. You can't think you'll get away with this."

"Please do. I am looking out for your welfare. Something you don't seem capable of doing."

Her mouth drops open and she glares at me.

"I am perfectly capable. As I said before, I am wearing sunscreen, you imbecile."

"Yes. I could smell it on you. Coconut tanning oil is not the same as sunscreen. And I can't say spending copious amounts of time in the sun after drinking alcohol is any better." I chuckle.

"What the hell do you want from me, Dayton?" She throws her hands in the air as if giving up. "I'm here. I don't have a choice. I'd like to relax. And pretend like this is a vacation. Or something."

"It's not a vacation."

She looks at me with a softness I haven't seen.

"It is to me." Her voice quiets.

Every instinct in me is switched on at the broken tone that swayed me the night before—the part of her Zach counted on me being unable to refuse.

Because I want to reach for her, I shove my hands into my pocket. My voice is cold.

"I don't see how that's my problem."

"It's not."

She doesn't sound angry. The fire evident in her

movements, is gone. It makes me equally devoid of it . . . and swamped with guilt—highly irrational as I am only doing what is best for her.

Uncomfortable with the possibility of Esme crying, something I have no intention of witnessing, I roll my shoulders. Down the hall is my escape. "Stay out of the sun, Esme. Or put on something more substantial than that scrap of fabric you're wearing."

When the flicker returns in her eyes, guilt diminishes, and I silently congratulate myself before turning away. The heat of her gaze follows me long after I leave her.

I don't see her for four days.

And with each day I don't see her, a new sensation of impatience and temper consumes me. I don't sleep. It's slightly comforting to imagine Esme not sleeping either. I doubt that to be the case.

As if given a perfect schedule to avoid one another, we pass like shadows in the house—once my haven. Now, it has become my own prison. And with me . . . an unwilling, infuriated, cohabitant.

I stare at the rocks below and the crashing waves, thinking over my plan as I do before a kill. I like to know the time, place, and intended victim as well as possible before completing a job. Not out of some sadist or masochistic drive, but for the simple urge to succeed—and live. Often, they go hand in hand.

My eyes close and I inhale deeply of brine and the fragrance of hibiscus. There's a large bush several feet below—the orange petals and yellow stamen reaching for the temperate sun. With such a tranquil and mild day, one would never guess it is October.

One reason I picked a place close to the equator, it tends to stay peacefully at around eighty degrees. Like finally given a mooring point, it has been a constant in my life—returning to the island and finding it just as I left it.

Until Esme.

Should a woman, a stranger . . . the daughter of my superior be so confounding? So disrupting?

With my eyes closed, I replay her face, those luminescent eyes and the wave of blond hair. It isn't because she's striking. Or has a voice like a sultry jazz singer. There is something else—something about that woman calls to me as a man. I am awake and reliving each second I've shared with her in my mission to eradicate this deep yearning. Because the truth is, when I saw her standing like a lost soul, drenched in moonlight . . . I knew there was something different about her. Something I should stay far away from.

My eyes open slightly in the bright light, and I sigh—with self-condemnation. I'm going to break our silent treaty and invite her to dinner.

I shouldn't. But I will.

I want to see her, to test myself . . . and her. I am a glutton for punishment to want to be near Esme, even knowing between us—there can be nothing.

God, I've lost my mind or am slowly going to.

This obsession that pervades every ounce of my carefully patch-worked life, is not just another disruption, it is quite possibly the beginning of my ruin, and that of Esme Costello. Where light and dark never meet—that's where Esme and I stand, and should remain. The fact that I've been thinking a lot about crossing that clearly marked barrier is absurd—and humbling—because I can't stop myself.

I spot Esme picking her way along the rocks at the edge of the water. Her hair is loose and frivolous, her legs, beneath little blue shorts, are long and as pale as the sand. The woman appears to have no idea of her appeal, and what her scrimpy clothing does. Like adding frosting to an already mouthwatering dessert. It makes my stomach hurt.

It seems God has given me the opportunity to do exactly as I wanted to. And I am rooted to the spot like a frightened little boy. A sensation I resent.

My chance to leave ends when Esme looks up to the sandy dunes and sees me.

We stare at one another like shy children. My feet are moving me closer without my permission. I stop a good distance from her. My ability to speak is intact—at least partially.

"I told you to check in with me when you leave the house."

My chiding is weak. I don't think she can tell.

"This is me checking in then. I'm going to be out all day. Exploring."

I look at my sand covered feet. I've never been uncomfortable around the opposite sex. I have a reputation for having a string of them running after me. I pride myself in my ability to treat a woman with the respect she deserves and the romance she wants. In Esme's case, I've treated her no better than I might an annoying insect. As to romance, there should be none, so at least there I have succeeded. I have no idea how I manage to do so. The woman has an uncanny ability to get under my skin and twist me around as if I'm her marionette.

I glance at those sinfully long legs—strictly for inventory purposes. She is healthy . . . and lovely.

"I haven't seen you in days. Are you at least feeding yourself?"

"Yes."

Her smile is pert.

"And I can dress myself all on my own too. Isn't it wonderful? Somehow, being an adult makes me able to do things I never dreamed possible. Without having my every action supervised."

I accept her sarcasm, and try to restrain an admiring

grin. I've always enjoyed dry humor. And hers comes easily.

"I'm glad to see you're settling in well then. But seeing as I haven't actually seen you eating meals and caring for yourself, I'm insisting you join me for dinner tonight."

Smooth. My interest is hidden, I'm not asking—I'm telling.

Her eyes narrow. If she sees the sweat growing on my face, she doesn't say so.

"I don't think that's necessary."

I step closer. Esme smells like some French dream, bathed in rose petals and crème. It makes my hands itch to do things and I clamp them into fists.

"I do. I cook well and would like to at least see one good meal make its way into you. From what I can tell, you've only made soup or put together a sandwich before skulking off into your room. That's hardly good enough to pass as proper nutrition."

At her continued glare, I raise my eyebrows. "Is my company so repulsive you'd skip having Coq au Vin?"

"Is it Julia Child's recipe?"

She knows the dish. I hoped it would entice her. I intend to feed her rooster, smothered in red wine sauce, bacon, butter and beef stock, over a candlelit dinner. Such a meal should smooth out any ill-feelings between us from the pool incident. I realize how romantic my intended setting may be. I'm reckless enough not to care.

"*Oui.* I imagine you've tasted a version or two of it. But I have been taught by the best." I do not mention the best is her father. Zach is never far from a kitchen or a good pairing of wine and cheese. He is French to his core.

I see she is considering her options, weighing her dislike with me for a chance to eat something other than canned soup. When she faces me, I can tell Esme has decided to accept. Victory is sweet! I relax a little.

"What time?"

"Six. I'll be making an appetizer and pouring a favorite blush wine of mine. I can promise you'll enjoy it."

"Why are you being nice to me, Dayton?"

"I'm not sure I'd call it that."

I haven't figured it out yet, except I need to be around her. To see and speak and understand how she's bewitched me in this last week of our stalemate. The rest, I will work through when the time comes. If not, I'm sure Zach will be of great use in knocking some sense into me.

Her eyes light with humor. It makes my stomach knot.

"Well, whatever you'd like to call it Dayton, cooking a woman a meal is considered nice. If not, romantic. Are you putting the moves on me?"

"If I were, you wouldn't need to ask. Dinner is at six. Don't get lost on the island, *snoepje*."

I head for the house, she mumbles about men being stubborn pigs. Maybe she knew I called her a piece of candy. I do smile, but not where she can see. I give her advice I'm sure she can use on her adventures. "Watch out for   snakes."

Her   growl   warms   me   immensely.

Chapter 4 *Confessions over Dinner*

Esme

So it is to be dinner with the oaf. Fine!

I can cope with an obnoxious, overbearing mule whilst eating his fancy cooking. Drinking his wine and enjoying his appetizer will be quite palatable.

He prepares dinner nightly, and has been torturing me with the smells of cooking for the last four days.

Walking through palm fronds and overgrown branches, sweat trickles down my spine and I welcome it. I need the air in my lungs and the clear sky without the constraint of walls. After the pool incident, I decided living in my room might be the best option as opposed to ever seeing Dayton again.

I gave up within a day and altered my plans to simply skulking about and avoiding any overlap in his presence. Which worked until today

Stopping to catch my breath, I frown at a line of red ants marching while carrying crumbs or something, and decide they would be good listeners. "What the hell does 'snoopeeya' mean?" I gesture at them. "Some terrible Dutch insult? I'm going to have to look it up now. Pig."

If I close my eyes, I'm certain I can recall every line

and mark on that man's face. I froze to the spot when we saw each other. Worse, I was happy to see him after so many days of 'what if' scenarios traipsed through my head. I've spent countless hours with only myself for company and a deserted island for scenery. Of course, I was happy to see a living breathing person. I enjoy spending time alone. I often relish it. But this sort of isolation from the world, is more like a jail than a sanctuary. It's the only reason I felt relief when I saw Dayton on the beach.

I stop at a large boulder to rest and peer at the island.

Who am I kidding?

I wasn't happy to see just anyone. I was happy to see Dayton. His eyes take me in with that chill I'm warming to. And that face—made for sculptures. Especially with his larger-than-life size. Dayton is without a doubt, the most compelling man I've ever met, and the most frightening. And yet, here I am, sweating and frustrated because I accepted his dinner invitation and now I'm not sure how to behave around him.

He's rude. Insolent. Certainly arrogant . . . dangerous.

I like him.

That's the God's honest strange truth. I'm drawn to his attitude and gruff way of speaking to me. Is it because he is so different from Carl? Because Dayton says what he thinks no matter how it might sound? I dread comparing the men, but it's impossible not to. Carl, my first real relationship, is the measuring stick I'm afraid I will use in the future. I wish his memory would die.

I ignore the lump in my throat and smile at the ants, who I'm sure are riveted to my words. "He's nothing like Carl."

I take their silence as agreement. "Dayton is cold and abrasive. He's outright rude and not in the least, a gentleman. Carl on the other hand, was opposite. It attracted me. He was suave and gentle, polite and full of compliments. He said and did all the right things . . . and in the end, was the monster of legends. If Dayton is nothing like that to begin with, what does that say about him?" My voice trails off and my audience has dwindled to a few ants who feverishly gather morsels from the black dirt.

I need a woman to talk things over with. No, I shake my head, mopping my head with a handkerchief, I need a shopping trip. And a woman for company. And a tall, very cold Bellini.

Speaking to ants is a new low.

Depressed at the thought, I give up on the rest of my exploring for the day.

I walk the half-trodden path back. The picture of the house perched on the hill is a welcoming sight. It's only been a week. And it's more like home than any house I've ever lived in.

I laugh, giving into my silly side and run for the waves lapping at the base of the long posts of the house. The water rushes over my legs, sucking at my toes and splashes me. I love it.

Wading deep enough till it comes to my top, I make several mermaid-style dives and come up laughing when a wave knocks me back under.

I have not had enough simple, or silly—or carefree.

I need more of it in my life. And far less of things that threaten to depress me till I'm ninety.

I can thank Zachariah for giving me that at least.

When I scramble up the banks and make my way toward the house, I'm weighted by my sticky clothes, but lighter in spirit. I can handle anything. Including my strange attraction to Dayton.

I shower, slather on my favorite rose lotion and slide into a soft sunset colored dress. It matches my gently growing tan and compliments my hair when I style it. Until I see my reflection in the long mirror, I'm unaware I'm getting ready as if for a date

I'm dressed casually, but with the mascara and the cheery lipstick, it appears like I dressed to impress.

I suppose maybe I did.

But I look happy. And that should matter most, shouldn't it? I walk barefoot into the hall toward the smell of food. I can hear the sizzle before I see the chef.

Dayton is at the kitchen island, his hands effortlessly slicing thick wedges of melon. It makes my mouth water. I haven't eaten since breakfast. It becomes common knowledge when my stomach growls louder than the homey sounds produced on the stove.

He surprises me with a good-natured smile. It transforms his face from dark and brooding to starkly handsome. His eyes linger on mine, fall to my dress then back to the melon in his hands.

"I'm glad you are hungry. I'm finishing the drinks. Melon spritzers."

"Alcoholic?"

He smirks.

"Just checking."

"Of course. I assume you like melon?" His eyes roam over me, around me, then seem to look through me as he resumes his work.

"Yes. I worked up quite the appetite trudging around the island. Can I help you with anything?" I'm disappointed he didn't mention how I look. I guess I am somewhat vain.

Dayton pauses, apparently taking stock of his tasks. "Yes actually. I could use another pair of hands. Can you make a salad? Cut romaine and spinach?"

I nod. He raises his eyebrows, and rummages in the refrigerator.

His voice is muffled coming from inside the fridge. "Cut the romaine into bite size pieces and the spinach a little smaller. Grate the Asiago finely then toss it together with these croutons and this peppercorn dressing."

I step to my station and accept the knife he offers me. "Do you always cook so extravagantly? Or am I getting something special tonight?"

Dayton looks at me. His assessment makes me want to squirm.

"I suppose the truthful answer is both. I enjoy cooking. It's a distraction from my work outside the island. And, in a way, I'd like to use this meal as a peace offering."

"An olive branch . . ." I lift a bit of spinach and twirl it. "Or leaf."

"Yes. It's hardly ideal to live together and be on such poor terms."

So, this is merely a way to keep the peace between us, not an apology. It's extremely tempting to ask him if my father has anything to do with his change of heart, but I don't really want to know. I don't want to spoil the evening or my appetite. I wish to have fun. To forget why I need fun and forgetfulness in the first place.

After a few minutes of slicing and silence, my shoulders relax and my hands are steadier as I dice and chop. When the bowl is filled with green, croutons and cheese, I use the offered tongs and toss it together. It smells glorious.

"What did you do with yourself before coming to the island, Esme?"

I leave the Zen. An odd way of phrasing that question. Though, Dayton is exactly what I classify as an odd man.

"I worked. For a lucrative modeling firm based out of Amsterdam, as the vice president."

"That explains the clothes."

He offers me a melon colored drink in a tall glass. A piece of honey dew and cantaloupe dress the top like a bow with a spear through it.

"Wearing the merchandise is part of the perks. Yes, I like fashion. And it likes me. I'd ask about your profession, but I don't think you want to talk about it yet."

Dayton samples the drink. He wanders out to the terrace. The sun is sinking. I follow him and settle a safe distance away against the coppery railing.

"I can't talk about something I know your father hasn't spoken to you about. Although, I think it would be best if you knew."

"I know whatever you two do, it isn't legal, at least not entirely. I know my father isn't a saint."

"None of us are."

This is dangerous territory. I tread carefully.

"It bothers you, doesn't it?"

"What does?"

There's the abrupt sense of walls dropping into place.

I gesture toward the water. "Whatever you do outside of this place. It weighs on you. Otherwise you wouldn't have built a way to escape all of it to the extreme of buying your own island."

"You're very perceptive, and bold."

"A curse, I've been told. But it's easy enough to see you aren't happy with my father. And I'm thinking it's not just because of me."

His eyes tell me I've hit a mark, and I stiffen before I can stop the fear. Dayton is not Carl. And not all men become violent when questioned.

His jaw flexes. "What else do you do besides modeling and psychoanalyzing?"

I take his shot with a grin and lean on the rail, my insides loosening from their pain.

"I don't model. I run the modeling. And I'm sorry if I poked a nerve." His silence urges me to fill the space between us with something. Anything. "I like to paint. But I'm not particularly good at it. I have a room back in . . . "

I think of that elaborate home and abruptly wish I hadn't.

"In Amsterdam. I had a good hundred paintings stacked in. Like cooking for you, painting gave me an out. Even if it was silly when completed."

"I doubt anything you paint would be silly."

Such certainty even though he's never seen them. Carl told me the opposite so many times—I don't think I could handle a good critique of my work. But it's nice, just the same, to have Dayton's vote of confidence. Even if it is to keep the peace between us.

The timer goes off in the kitchen. Dinner must be done.

We go back into the kitchen. Dayton takes the casserole from the oven, while I nibble on a feta and garlic canape. It's hard to resist grabbing a few before moving to the deck.

Dayton finishes setting the table, in his careful and strict way. He serves the coq au vin with the skill of a Cordon Bleu chef, ladling the rich wine sauce, on to two plates like an artist displaying his finest work. The salad is served separately. My curiosity about the man is exponentially growing.

He pulls out my chair. I feel my cheeks flush when he pushes it back in. Thankfully, he lets me place my own napkin in my lap. From hardly civilized brute to gentleman. The man has transformed and leaves me wondering if like a werewolf, he will change back when the full moon—just coming out for its duty in the stars—is over.

"It tastes divine. You cook wonderfully."

"I enjoy it," he says this with his gaze riveted to the table.

"You don't take compliments well, do you?"

"Do you?"

"Yes, thank you. Compliments and nice things are very welcomed. But you're diverting from yourself. I notice you like doing that too."

"I notice you enjoy talking a lot. It's a wonder you manage to analyze those around you with how often your mouth is open."

The hint of irritation is back. I almost thought the growling bear was gone. This version of Dayton is far easier to handle and understand.

"Am I allowed to ask what you've been up to these last days? As a simple conversation starter."

"Working."

"On?"

Like pulling teeth. Beneath the soft silk of his shirt and expensive shoes, he's Dayton— the man who held a gun to my head a week ago and drug me from his pool like a barbaric ape.

He wipes his mouth. "I've been making plans to add on a guest house."

"That would certainly make things comfortable for you if you have company. What with your inability to share or . . . enjoy company at all."

"Yes."

He gives me a pointed look and I merely chew happily on my rooster. The sauce tastes like it was made by a guru of culinary arts. If I knew the man could cook so well, perhaps I'd sucked up to him for meals sooner. As it is, I plan on playing nice for the foreseeable future.

"How many rooms?"

"Three."

"Bathrooms?"

His mouth twitches—a sign of amusement I'm getting good at recognizing.

"Two."

"A cozy cottage then. You should put in a hot tub. That would be a nice touch for the guests."

"I have one already in the main-house."

I drop my fork. "Where? I haven't seen it."

"It's on the second floor. The roof."

"Ah, the forbidden floor. Well, in that case, you most definitely need a hot tub for the guest house. Unless you wish to threaten every guest in the same fashion you did me."

"And if I did?" He's playing with me. It makes my heart go unsteady and my breath uneven.

"I would make sure you have a good lawyer. Not everyone is as forgiving."

He laughs now. Warmth pools in me and makes my hands clumsy. Even if I wanted to finish eating, I can't now. Not with my nerves as they are. This side of Dayton is far too charming and—I'm too attracted to it.

"Well." I stand, and he stands with me. Ignoring him, I feign a yawn and place my hand on my stomach. "I couldn't eat another bite. Thank you for the meal. And I'm very tired. I think I'll call it a night. Mission accomplished. Peace has been restored throughout the land."

I say this with bland inflection. Dayton raises his arm to stop my exit, I look up at him.

"Stay. Just a little longer."

My mouth is suddenly dry as a desert. "I suppose . . . I suppose I could."

He doesn't touch me, but I feel him as strongly as if he did. He guides me into the large sitting room. The open fireplace with an ornate mantel is empty now, but I can imagine it burning on a winter night—if this place ever got colder than seventy degrees.

We remain a safe distance apart. My end of the sofa is perfectly comfortable and I'm confident Dayton's is the same. Only now that the scent of food, and candlelight is gone, I am stiff as a board.

"I have news from your father."

His way of addressing this calms me.

"News? About Amsterdam?"

"*Oui*. He asked me to tell you things are progressing

as planned. He hopes an end will be forthcoming in a few weeks."

"Weeks?"

"It is what he said."

I jolt. My breath goes short for different reasons than before. Abruptly, I am brought back to a filigree encrusted bed, gilded mirrors and an armoire painted in antique yellow. Only there are speckles of blood on the yellow, and the brassy doorknob is smeared in violent red.

"What are you afraid of, Esme?"

"I'm not afraid."

"You've lost all your color. Your hands are clenched."

"I'm upset. It's a great many weeks to be away from work. I planned on returning faster."

"I was under the impression you may not ever be able to return to Amsterdam. Zach made it sound as if you had run out of options."

This is something I've thought of, but never seriously considered. My business is there. My life was there . . . and then everything crashed that night with Carl. Images flash in my mind and I force them out. I will not be dragged down again. I can't think of that. It's done. He's done. Why can't I make him leave me be?

Whatever my father needs to do—whatever needs to take place, it won't change that Carl can never come for me. He's dead.

My father and I know it won't end until his family is dealt with. I don't particularly wish to know the ways in which Zachariah is doing it, or the problem he thinks will only need a few weeks.

"It's one scenario."

"Esme . . .?"

"Don't ask me what happened, Dayton. I won't answer you. I can't."

"Because of your father?"

"Some of it is. He told me not to be speaking to anyone about it. There are things that make my situation delicate."

"Things Zachariah doesn't want me to know."

"Yes. I think so. He wasn't clear. But that isn't the point."

I'm feeling anxiety and guilt. "I got myself into something. And I couldn't find a way out until too late. Zachariah, is helping me with that. And I'm sorry he is using you to help too, but I can't be sorry I'm here."

"I'm not sorry."

I glance over my shoulder. Dayton is standing so close to me now a whisper could separate us. A whisper or a kiss. He might kiss me. And worse, I want him to. Even if I'm fairly certain, I would be using him just to escape the reality of the nightmare I've gotten myself into.

"Ghosts haunt your eyes."

His fingers brush my shoulder blade, like angel wings.

"Dayton . . .?" I turn, expecting him to speak. But he doesn't say anything, he merely watches me, his eyes tracing my face before his fingers touch where his eyes were.

"You are lovely. You've gotten more sun."

"I like the sun."

His smile is warm. It's like being drugged from the inside out.

"Too much I think."

I don't tell him I can do whatever I want. Dayton's eyes are too soft. Too rich for me to turn away.

"You should go to bed now, Esme."

"I could . . ." I'm stalling.

"Goodnight."

Like a brother kissing a little sister, he leans forward, presses his lips to my forehead. Then kisses my warm cheeks as a farewell.

I'm mortified. I practically threw myself at him. And here he kisses me, as if I'm a tiny dove he thinks to mend. That is exactly what I am to him.

"Yes, well, goodnight."

It sounds cold. Formal. I can't say anything else. Ignoring the impulse to run to my bedroom, I walk, however without leisure, directly to my room. When I close myself off from the fragrant food and wine, I sink to the bottom of my door.

"What is wrong with me?"

I sigh from sheer exhaustion. I refuse tears. I don't get up until my body can no longer handle the hard floor. I climb into bed fully dressed. I don't sleep well. The nightmares cling to me, with Carl's whitewashed face sneering above me.

Chapter 5 *Warming Waters*

Esme

Another week passes on the island and I'm beginning to hit my stride.

I walk, swim, or visit the gym daily—during the allotted hours. It helps to focus my mind and is great for my burgeoning waistline. I love food . . . so I must exercise. I wish it were the other way around.

I stand in front of my mirror, in my matching underwear and bra, a deep aqua overlaid in lace, and I look good. Really good.

I haven't felt like this since before Amsterdam. My days in London are a vague memory, amidst the solitude of the island.

I dress in canvas shorts with a billowing pale blue top. Daisies circle the hemline and short fluttery sleeves. As I am unabashedly prone to whimsy, I like to picture myself as some sort of fey goddess dressed in her casual beach attire.

It helps to bolster one's pride every now and then.

I laugh as I fluff my hair with the blow-dyer. I apply just a little makeup, going with the au naturel look today.

I'm not dressing to impress anyone. Not really.

I leave my room and head to the kitchen. It's empty, with the lingering smell of dark coffee and cinnamon. A lemon yellow dish with a fat cinnamon roll is beside a half-full coffee pot. In neat block letters, a neutral message printed on a sticky note reads, *Leftover from breakfast. Enjoy.* There is definitely peace in the land.

Placing a hand on my flat stomach, I will enjoy it.

Biting into the cinnamon roll is without a doubt, the best reward for jogging two miles and doing all of my abdominal routine. Although, whilst doing my crunches I cursed the person who created them to boil in a pot of acid.

The rest of my day is like the previous. I don't see Dayton. I don't even hear him. It's as if I'm living alone in this huge beach house on this deserted island with this breathtaking view.

But I don't mind. I love all the peace and quiet.

I peruse the study for the umpteenth time, and all of Dayton's books. Which consist of every non-fiction book a man could want. And not one single fictional feel-good story. I sip on my mug of green tea, tempted to see how I might order a few books via Amazon. Maybe they'd deliver to the island?

Rolling my eyes at the impossibility, I settle into a large pinstriped arm chair and sigh dramatically. "He needs a dog. Or a cat. Hell, even a fish."

"I'm partial to dogs."

I jerk, spill my tea on my lap and shriek as the scalding liquid burns through my shorts. Dayton's figure darkens the doorway. Everything about him is expressionless but his eyes. They dance.

"I now have second degree burns on my legs thanks to you."

"I'll get you some ice."

"No!" I snap, dusting my hands uselessly on my shorts. He doesn't seem to notice I'm glaring at him. "What do you want?"

"I thought you'd like some company . . . you were talking to yourself about my lack of a pet."

"I was musing. That's different."

"I take it you wish I had a pet for your company."

"Maybe. I like dogs."

"Too much work. I'm never on the island for longer than a couple of weeks."

"You could bring it with you."

Dayton comes into the study, eyes reviewing everything as though he's taking a mental photograph of the room and its contents for possible use.

"Have you been enjoying yourself? I see you're making use of the gym and pool."

"Yes. I like to stay in shape. Within reason."

"Hmmm."

"Is that judgement I hear?"

"No. Musing. It's different. Would you like to change?"

"I suppose that might be more comfortable."

"I'll wait for you on the lower deck."

I stop at the door. "For what?"

"I'm going for a walk. I thought you'd like to know where the best seashells are."

So, the man has been watching me after all.

When I go to the beach, I come back with seashells. Some broken, others pristine, but loaded with sand. I wash them in warm soapy water, and put them in the sun on the upper deck to dry.

"I would. Thank you." I go change into dry shorts.

Dayton is waiting beside a bed overflowing with brilliant orange tiger lilies.

"Better?"

"Yes."

Our evening together and all of the romantic possibilities, thankfully, is far from my mind.

We walk in silence, the sun signals the waning of

day, and I keep pace with Dayton, with an ever-growing curiosity.

"Are you ever tired of your own company out here?"

"No."

He steps over a large volcanic-type rock and winds his way over dry grass. A tiny crab scuttles out of the way.

"I guess you must love the sun then . . . to have picked an island."

"Who doesn't? It's warm. Easy to dress for."

Such bland answers. But I know the man beside me to be capable of red-hot anger—of searing words. That day at the pool was not my imagination.

"Do you always answer questions with as little words as possible? Or is that just for my sake?"

Dayton looks at me as if seeing me for the first time. "I'm not particularly chatty."

"And I am."

"Yes."

"Does that bother you about me? That I like to talk a lot?"

"I haven't decided yet."

I wait until we walk parallel to the waves before speaking. I don't want to frighten off my only source of human conversation. Or let on I have feelings for him.

"Would it be okay to ask where you grew up?"

He sighs, bending to capture a fat clam shell from the waves. "I grew up in Amsterdam."

Yes, I assumed that from his Dutch accent. He looks the part as well with his deep tan and dark blond hair. But those eyes . . . the green is more merman than human. He'd laugh if he knew how often I picture them before going to sleep.

"I grew up in Chicago mostly. But ended up in Detroit for a time."

He hands me the shell and walks.

"What about your family? Do you have siblings? Were you an only child? Parents?"

He stops so abruptly I bump into him and work not to fall into the surf.

"Why are you asking me all these questions?"

"Because, it's normal to want to get to know the man taking care of you. We have only each other for company. And you suggested we get along. Why not . . . why not learn about each other?"

His eyes drop to my mouth then back to my eyes.

"There is nothing good to learn about. I am an only child. A neighbor raised me after my father died. I didn't have a pleasant childhood and I am already aware of your circumstances."

"Oh?"

"Your father included a personal history several days ago, for background."

My face warms when I think about things that may have been in that history. I need to call my father and explain to him about personal space and privacy.

"Well, that should only make things buzz right along between us."

"To what?"

"To . . . becoming friends."

Dayton smiles. I follow him with a sigh of relief. Perhaps it's been a long time since I've had the opportunity to interact with a person of the opposite sex who is not a Carl. Or Dayton Jepsen is a particularly difficult person to interact with—I'm going to say it's the latter.

I pick up a shell and offer it to Dayton. He accepts it without speaking.

"It's your turn to ask a question." I don't do well hiding the exasperation.

He sighs. "What would you like for dinner?'

"A real question."

"It is a real question Esme. I'd like to know what to cook. I have some Mahi-Mahi if you'd like."

"Don't you have anything you'd like to know? Any curiosities?"

I can see that damnable hint of amusement and I want to call him out on it . . . before the full smile.

"I know you get your impatience from your father."

"And my looks, from my mother. She's in prison for manslaughter. She's killed too."

His expression changes. "I don't think the kills are on the same level. However, I'd have to see your mother's particular case. Are you worried you are the same as her?"

"On some level, aren't I?"

"Why did she kill?"

I cross my arms. "For money. She fought with her fiancé. He lost."

"And you?"

His eyes are piercing. I think about it, and force myself to recall even for a second what I did.

"To live."

"Then you are not the same."

"As simple as that, huh?"

His eyes scan the horizon. "It is for those on the outside . . ." He glances back at me.

"What do you want for dinner?"

"Mahi-Mahi sounds good I guess."

Dayton laughs. "When I cook, it's always good."

There's that arrogance I enjoy.

Dayton

I'm playing a game. And losing.

I'm doing my best to ignore Esme, to not think of, worry over, or have anything—having to do with Esme.

And I am failing.

I fiddle with the old record player until Mozart floods the room. I'm not enjoying the fanciful sound of classical music, but don't care enough to change the vinyl. That requires I go into the study.

Meaning, I possibly run into and interact with Esme. Whom I'm not thinking of.

And I'm far too busy for that.

I open my email and file through the spam first, and delete a few hundred emails from random sources or names I don't recognize.

The rest, a total of five, are from either Zachariah or Jacque. I read Zach's and they are as expected. The first, a list of new contracts up for grabs, the second, upcoming training seminars. Third and fourth, how do you do, and when are you coming back queries. And the fifth, a quarterly newsletter on the corporation's overhead costs and budget to help choke the twenty-percent contract fee off the top of each kill.

I open Jacque's email and see his usual slapstick humor—a meme.

You can't spell assassin without sin . . . and twice the ass!

STOP FOOLING AROUND AND GET BACK TO WORK.

-J

I close my laptop, and spend the rest of the afternoon considering the contracts Zach sent. I read a few, but I'm not compelled to claim dibs on any. It isn't as though I need the money. Or I don't have the time. Though, I am rather busy with my current position as babysitter.

I should hit the gym. Or file the last year of contracts I have in a pile. Hell, I should call Zach and tell him to send someone else to play caretaker to his lustrous daughter because I've got important work to do.

Instead, I leave my desk. My feet tingle from sitting

so long. Darkness has descended over the island while I was lost in thought.

I want to see what is growing between Esme and me. But upon further review, it is simply poor deduction on my part. I don't need to know. I already know what is brewing. I need to steer clear and keep my head down. Friendliness aside, I need to get out of this thing all pieces accounted for. Most especially that precious organ I have to remind myself on occasion I do actually have.

I take stairs down to the kitchen.

Here, the place is as uncomplicated as life ought to be. There are recipes for meals, spices to change or alter, ingredients to create new exciting tastes. A man could lose himself for days in a well-stocked kitchen. I peruse the wine rack and settle on a merlot to cap the night off. With Havarti and crackers, it is a fine meal.

I sit at the bar with my makeshift supper, sipping wine and tasting cheese . . . thinking.

I catch a shimmer on the beach and I'm aware I'm enjoying not only the scenery.

Esme is wading in the surf, underneath alabaster moonlight, her face tipped back as if to soak up the beams. I choke on my cracker. I gulp my wine to save me.

The idea of avoiding her, of heading upstairs to bed disappears when I watch her. Esme is a siren, not simply a woman.

I step into the balmy night. The wind is rough and pulls at my clothes. The air smells ripe with electricity. It will storm tonight.

I wait until Esme faces me . . . wait until those moonstone eyes peer at me from across the beach to say anything. When she merely waits in the water, her hair blowing wildly, I close the distance. If I believed in magic like that of Merlin, I'd think Esme a sorceress.

"Smells like rain."

She tries to tame her hair.

"Yes. It does. Is there something you needed?"

I watch her—try not to see everything about her. I see everything. I don't want to, and feel twice as much. I pull my gaze away and can just make out the spears of waves reaching for the sky. Lightning flashes ominously above us and Esme flinches.

"Maybe you should go inside. Standing out here we're likely to get hit by lightning."

Esme edges closer. "I doubt that. It's heat lighting."

It cuts wicked fingers in the sky followed by rumbling thunder. She jumps.

"You were saying?"

"Don't be an ass."

Trying not to laugh, I take Esme's hand and jog back. We reach the walk-out at the same time the heavens open and we're pelted with raindrops the size of kiwis. Esme laughs and surprisingly, I do too as we make our way out of the deluge and up the steps to the main floor.

With the house dark and the rain pounding overhead, standing close to Esme is particularly tempting . . . and wrong.

"I'll get you a towel."

I head for the bath off the hallway and get two navy towels, taking a minute longer to chastise myself at getting swayed by the moment. Esme turns on several lights in the kitchen and living area. She stands like a pitiful drowned rat.

"Here." I offer her a towel and step back to dry myself.

Esme is first to break the silence . . . softly.

"Have you ever been married?

I stop toweling. "No. Have you?"

"No."

"Ever been in love?" Esme bites her lower lip, drying her hair with the towel.

"I shouldn't answer that."

"Because you've been in love before?"

"No, because I haven't. And I'm not likely ever to be."

She drapes the towel around her shoulders. "I don't think I've ever been in love before either. But I hope one day I could be."

"You're the type who believes in fairy tales."

"And you aren't."

"I'm a realist."

"Or a pessimist."

I'm suddenly awkward, damn it, unsure of myself. What the hell does she do to me, to make me feel so bloody out of my element? I don't fumble with women. I don't stare at them stupidly and I most certainly don't answer personal questions. But over the last days, I've done all of those things and I'm getting tired of it.

"I should get to bed. Got an early day. Work to do."

"What sort of work?"

I frown at Esme. Her eyes like heated blue gems on me. It aggravates me further. "Just work, Esme. You don't need to know everything about me."

I have to smother the urge to swear. "I'm sorry. I'm only asking to be friendly."

"Then don't be so friendly with me."

"Didn't you, come outside with me? Weren't you the one to suggest we get along and have peace?"

She seems confused. I don't blame her. I am being confusing.

"Yes, well, maybe I was wrong."

Esme's eyes are fiery. If she knew how close I am to kissing her, she might run. She should. Because it won't be gentle and it most certainly won't be the end of it.

"Maybe you were. But I don't see the point in being a world-class jerk when it's your mistake—not mine. If you don't want to be nice to me, or be friendly, then stop showing up. Stop making yourself available to me."

I'm closer. Her eyes have rounded and her hands fisted. I shouldn't frighten her. But I can't help it.

"Listen, it's my house. It's my space. If I end up running into you, it is not, by any means, me making myself available to you."

"You like pushing at me because it keeps me at arms distance."

I settle for sarcasm instead of rage. "Yes, exactly. Bravo for your incredible deductive skills."

"I'm not buying it."

Esme closes that blasted gap between us and I can smell the rain on her skin. It's dizzying.

"What are you so scared of? That you might actually like me? Because I'm a pretty likeable person."

"Damn it Esme." I grasp her arms, shove her back a few steps and inhale a gallon of air as quickly as possible. "Just . . . give me some space. I don't like to be pushed."

"Clearly. You like pushing."

"That's correct. And it suits me. Don't go rearranging things. You won't like what you find. Or what I become."

"I'm not as weak as you think. And from the sound of it, you aren't as strong."

Before I can come up with something better to say, she twirls on her heel and heads to the hall.

"Goodnight Dayton. We'll see how tomorrow goes."

Chapter 6 *Breaking Rules*

Esme

"Yes, Dayton has been a good host."

There is a pause before Zachariah replies. "I'm sure he has. Have you been taking care of yourself? Enjoying the island?"

I sink into the pillows. "Yes. As much as one can. Why have you called?"

"Am I not allowed to check on my only child?"

I can't be angry with him for never knowing about me until two years ago. Beneath my cheerfulness resentment lingers. I wish it didn't. Growing up in the American foster system, I have my share of sob story child horrors and learned to begrudge the biological family I believed had given me up. In truth, only my mother signed away her rights after they sent her to prison, and my birth certificate did not list my father.

Several years into my emancipation, I hired a private investigator, spent every scrap of money from questionable jobs, and found Zachariah Moncleve as the likeliest candidate for my father. His photograph convinced me. I don't think I look remotely related, but his smile is mine.

I sent a letter. And waited, wracked with indecision, concerned about what he might think. That he would dismiss my claims and ignore me. By all rights, he should have. Who accepts a daughter conceived through a few grubby nights in a motel?

But that wasn't the case.

After moving from London to Amsterdam as vice president in the Magnifique Modeling Agency, Zachariah—my father—found me. He offered to get to know me . . . to build a relationship. It should have made me grateful for the chance to forge family ties. But with my hidden resentment, I quickly discovered, I am wary. Family isn't something I understand well.

I accepted his invitation with the stipulation we begin by mail.

Two years later, we never made it past written correspondence . . . entirely by my choice. But I had never been happier in my life than to pick up that paper he gave me with his phone number in case I were to have a change of heart. Now, speaking with him on the phone as though we actually know one another is strange. In some ways, I do know him. In others, he is as much a stranger to me as any person walking by.

"Esme?"

I realize how long I remained silent. "I'm not a child. Zachariah. There is no need to treat me like one."

His laugh is rich, and gentle in response. It creates a strange longing. And I wonder what might have been, had my mother offered him a chance to care for me instead of the path I ended up on.

"That you aren't. Listen, I'm not calling for a chance to check on you. I have word from my connections in Amsterdam. There is movement within the ranks of the Tormina family. I don't need to tell you we are monitoring this, and I am keeping a close eye on your safety. But, I have also spoken to Dayton about it. He suggests I send an extra man for security. I have to say, I agree."

"He knows then, about the Tormina family and Carl?"

"No."

"How could he not know? What are you hiding from him?" I have to will my heart to slow at the prospect of lying to Dayton. "I have a right to know. Perhaps he does too."

The silence from Zachariah denotes guilt. Or an admission of some small part. "He isn't ready to hear it. Not yet. Dayton is also connected to the Tormina family in a way that could jeopardize his position in my company."

So many secrets. So many lies. I hate it.

"So it's money-based."

"Of course not, Esme. Dayton is like a son to me. But he is, absolutely one of the best in the business. And I'm aware he'd like to retire soon. Which will require anonymity if he is do it in peace. His life before he joined me, connects him to the Tormina family—specifically Molin Tormina. I need you on this to make sure things run smoothly."

"What are you going to do? How are you going to help me out of this?" My voice is paper thin. "Are you planning on assassinating the entire Tormina family to protect me?"

The words sound ridiculous, and a bit dramatic.

His sigh is audible. "Esme, my darling, I will do as I must. I have only just found you. And you are young. What you did to protect yourself, is something I will be forever proud of. But it means, as your father, whether or not you like it, you must trust me to care for you in this. I may not be a good man, but I am good at what I do. And so is Dayton. Give me a little time, and I'll explain it all."

"To Dayton?"

It matters more to me now than it did two weeks ago. Has it already been two weeks on this island?

"To both of you. I've given what information I can to Dayton—without alerting him to who I am involved with. He knows it is a wealthy crime family in the Amsterdam syndicate. He also knows you killed a key member and are now threatened with your life. The rest, the details of who, will come later when I solidify the plan to stop the threat. These things must be dealt with quietly. And carefully."

Or else Interpol will find him. And me.

My stomach cramps thinking of what my father intends to do, and worse, how I'm going to sit quietly while he does it. What does he do for a living? I think he's already told me without telling me. I am physically ill.

"Jacque, my right hand, will be there by tomorrow. He is a trusted member of my company. And you can trust him. He and Dayton will take wonderful care of you. As for today, I've asked Dayton to take you to the mainland for some shopping. I think it might do you some good to get out."

I haven't been off the island since I got here. Shopping? Like a normal civilized person who has not a care in the world? I don't know if it's possible, but the desire to try rises. I hang onto it like a dying woman.

"Sure."

"Good, good. I've got a conference call with some associates in Guam in about ten minutes. I'll need to go over some figures before that. Will you be okay?"

"Yes."

"*Je t'aime, ma chérie.*"

I remember my high school French, and it makes my eyes sting. How a statement of love can mean so much from a stranger is beyond me, but it does. This man—my father—a criminal, like many of the men from my past, but the man who gave me life. It has to mean something. I inhale softly and do my best to sound calm.

"*Merci, mon père.*"

I hang up before I can hear his response. I don't want to know. I'm too busy trying to wrap my head around things. And the best way I can see to do that, is exactly as Zachariah suggested—go shopping. Act normally. Count the seconds until I can end the charade and try to go back to my life, or whatever is left of it.

I pull on jean shorts and a pale pink t-shirt with the Eiffel Tower on it. The soft cotton reminds me of home, warm on my cool skin.

I visit the kitchen, Dayton is in canvas shorts and a salmon button-down, and Corona flip-flops. I smile even though there's a sliver of trepidation. If my father is the man I think he is, then Dayton is too.

Even thinking those words feels like an admission of crime.

"Why are you looking at me like that?"

"Like what?" I side-step Dayton to find a protein bar. I'm not particularly hungry, but it gives me something to do. If I look too long at Dayton he might notice I'm unsettled after my conversation with Zachariah. Worse, he might see my thoughts—as I feel them.

"You spent a good deal of time on the phone with your father. I assume you've been updated as to the change of plans. Jacque will be flying in tomorrow and we'll probably see him by dinner."

"Oh yes, we talked about that."

Dayton's brows furrow, as I pick at the wrapper on the bar.

"Is there something you'd like to say to me?"

"Not particularly."

Suddenly, I'm not peering at my sandals but at flip-flops. Dayton's anger at my obvious evasion should scare me, with what I do know about him—but it doesn't.

I've known bad men. I've killed one . . . but Dayton

doesn't seem like one. My father doesn't either. Where is the line between good and evil?

"Why aren't you looking me in the eyes, Esme?"

"I don't know."

"Don't you?"

"Stop. You're making me nervous." I shove at his chest—it's granite.

I've never been any good at hiding my feelings. I've never been any good at not stating the obvious. My black and white view of the world is challenged and I have no choice. If my father and this man are the killers I think they might be, then I have to know. I don't want to know. I can't help it, I have to know.

"What are you? What do you do for a living Dayton? I want to know. I can't pretend it isn't a problem. Or that I'm not aware of something sinister going on."

"I told you I wouldn't talk about that until your father did."

"I know. He talked to me, sort of. And I need to hear it from you. I can't quite understand it. So, I need to hear it."

I am like an executioner asking for a statement of innocence from his intended victim. But Dayton is no victim.

A shadow passes in his eyes, maybe regret, and I know, it's true. My wild assumptions, my fears, my reality, just got stranger and far more dangerous. Dayton Jepsen, the man who has been living with me for the last two weeks, is a murderer. Like me.

"If you can't understand I'm a killer for hire, then I don't know what else me saying will help you."

"I . . . I didn't think . . . I"

The truth has run me over.

"Yes Esme, I kill for money. Mercenary. Assassin. Killer for hire. Whatever you like to call it. I execute national or foreign hits if the Phantoms offer the contract.

My numbers are good. Hell, I've got great numbers. I'd argue I'm the best in the business."

His eyes belie the anger in his voice. "Only rules I've got—I don't kill kids. And I have to know why I'm doing it. If it isn't a good enough reason, I don't take the contract."

"So you're a killer with morals?"

He laughs and it's as bitter as I expect an assassin to sound after years of . . . doing the job.

"Sure. You could call it that. Are you happy now? Anything else you'd like to know?"

"No.

"Are you sure? I don't want you wondering or being curious without answers. I'm happy to give you a list of my credentials or resume."

"Stop it."

"Stop what?"

"I wanted to know, yes, but you don't have to make it more crude than it is. You don't need to be cruel."

"Lady, I am cruel. I was born into it and I'm a product of it."

"I don't believe you. You don't like it."

"Wrong. I love the money. I love the freedom."

Now I'm backing him into the kitchen island. "No. You might like what it's gotten you in life, but you don't like it. You hate it. It eats at you. You told me there were ghosts in my eyes—there is a ghost. The man I killed. We both know I did, regardless of my reasons, it feels wrong in my head. He haunts me in my sleep."

Dayton's anger is palpable, too late to stop now. "I've got news for you, you've got ghosts in your eyes too, Dayton. I don't know how many. I don't need to know. All I need to know is right there. They haunt you. All of them. It's why you built this damn island and it's why you're hiding from my father out here. Because you aren't going back, are you?"

I'm out of breath now, my face undoubtedly tomato red, and I'm toe to toe with a man who outweighs me and out matches me on every level. A proclaimed killer. I'm either mad, out of my mind, or about to be.

I challenge him, yell at him, and poke my finger in his face. Overpowered by the sudden strength of an old but familiar version of myself, I don't stop. I have walked straight into a situation where Dayton can only be expected to react. I brace myself as I finish speaking.

The man crushes his mouth to mine, in a brutal, toe-curling, earth-shattering lip-lock.

I don't have the wherewithal to squirm, or to do anything but accept the harsh kiss and although I think he means to punish me, there is warmth behind his anger. His hands are tight on my upper arms, tight enough they might leave marks. I let him kiss me. I kiss him back—it's equally without gentleness.

Stopping abruptly, Dayton lifts me out of his way and stalks out of the room. Mouth swollen, lips tingling, I'm in a mental haze until he comes back into the room.

"I'm not waiting around all day for you. Hurry up, or get left behind. Our ride is here."

"Our ride?" My voice is rough.

"Yes. We're going to the mainland."

Chapter 7 *Punta Cana*

Dayton

Esme sits opposite me in a booth so frayed the upholstery should have been replaced a decade ago. The air is rich with aromas of chilies, Tostones, Sancocho, and Arroz Blanco. All favorites when coming to this little dive restaurant in Punta Cana. Seeing Esme here, in a place that has sentimental value to me, adds to the headache growing at the base of my skull.

I was a fool to grab her. To kiss her like some barbarian and to do it not out of simple want—there was plenty—but out of anger. Out of frustration at hearing all of the things I've already thought of. She hit the nail on the head dead on.

But that's not the only reason I'd been angry.

"Are we going to pretend that kiss didn't happen?"

Of course she is going to ask. Of course she can't let it go. God, how could I?

"Yes."

"I don't see how that's going to be possible," Esme says like a teacher reprimanding a naughty student.

"It is."

I flip open the plastic covered menu. It is in Spanish. I speak well enough to pick my way through and order. Tipping well usually results in better meals and service. Ignoring Esme's diamond-hard gaze, I raise my hand, and notice Erma, the busty waitress from my last visit, already sauntering over. She's twice my age, but has a soft spot for me.

Today, I welcome the distraction. *"Hola, ¿cómo es mi mujer favorita en toda Punta Cana?"*

She grins, propping a tray on her hip. I don't explain the menu to Esme, instead, I order her the same meal as myself. Sancocho and Arroz Blanco. We'll save the Tostones for last, if she's hungry enough. There is nothing like a fried plantain authentically cooked.

"¿Las bebidas habituales?"

Alcohol can do nothing but help the situation. *"Si. Dos."*

We pass the time in silence until Erma brings two margaritas and a bowl of chips hot from the fryer. I dig in and don't speak, knowing Esme will.

"We need to talk about this."

"I'm eating. You should too. The chips are delicious. The margaritas—" I gulp a mouthful of icy lime and tequila. "They hit the spot."

"You kissed me."

I'm hoping she can't see how badly I want to do it again. "Yes. You made me angry and I responded."

"By kissing me?"

I ignore the flutter in my stomach. "Yes, well, it shut you up, didn't it? I'm wondering if I should do it again."

Her cheeks redden. It is far more charming than it should be. The woman not only picked my life and profession apart, but she did a hell of a lot of peering into a place no one is welcome—my heart.

And I'll be damned if I'll admit how right she is about it all. I scorch my throat with another mouthful of chips and burning salsa.

"The chips really are good."

"Yes they are. Ever been to the Caribbean before?"

"No."

"Hispaniola is arguably the best island. Aside from my own."

Esme is scanning the restaurant. "Is there a name for your island? Or is it just, Dayton's Island?"

"I never thought of giving it a name."

"You should call it something."

"Come up with a name and I'll consider it."

She doesn't say anything else until the food arrives. We spend most of our time eating and conversing with small talk, which I don't care for. Most especially when I know her eyes are probing every time she thinks I'm not looking.

But I am.

When we finish, I do what Zach asked. I take her shopping. This brings Esme back to her usual self. Perhaps too much so.

Staring at the five hundredth scarf of the day, I run my hands over the silken fabric for the vendor, who prattles a price far too high, Esme says.

The woman is choosey. Who am I to try and control her?

I doubt anyone could.

She buys rings. Sandals. Scarves, and another swimsuit smaller than the red one. By the end of the fourth hour, my feet are aching and I swear if I don't get aspirin in me, I'm going to throat punch the next barefoot kid that begs me to buy beads.

"Having fun yet?"

Esme watches me. Having used me to carry her purchases, she is blissfully unencumbered and at some point bought some ice cream. It's laughable that I haven't the slightest idea when or where that happened. But it's the same color pink as her shirt and she looks achingly innocent eating it.

I frown. "Is there a stop button on you? Or should I give you a good shake and see if that slows you down?"

When she merely grins, I shake my head, because I want to smile back. Seconds earlier I contemplated throat punching children. The woman is a witch.

"Haven't you had any fun yet?"

I think of the various vendors and stores we've been into and do my best to find this fun Esme is speaking of.

"No."

She scowls at me. "You enjoyed when that street performer played so well for us. I didn't even have to give him money. You did."

I remember. He is very talented on the mandolin and yes, I was impressed. But that was eons ago. "I'm afraid your voracity for shopping has drowned out that particular memory. I can see why Zach thought you'd enjoy this. You look more alive than since I met you."

"Oh—thank you?"

Beyond her shoulder is the edge of the water. Already, it's as though the island is calling me home. As if I am its guardian and it needs me to survive—a warming thought that makes me ready to be rid of civilization.

"I can promise you it is a compliment. But it's been a day and I promised Janu I would return by five." I glance at my watch and feign a flinch. "My god, you've had me running all over Punta Cana for four and a half hours."

She rolls her eyes and trashes her ice cream. Punta Cana is fabulous this time of day. The sun is too warm, and the smell of food is rich. Yes, the vendors can be pushy and the sights can be overrun with tourists and noise, but the colors are vibrant. The homes, small and friendly, and the people welcoming. If I weren't so averse to living in the vicinity of anything with a pulse, I'd choose to live here.

We're quiet as we walk back in the direction of the docks and I'm tempted to hold Esme's hand because it's as though I ought to. I don't. My hours shopping with Esme have given me plenty of time to get my head back on my shoulders and to remind myself of the control I am gifted. Esme is my employer's daughter, that's enough to bar her from my interest in itself, without the added advantage of her being vulnerable and off-limits. She is a snag I don't need. A complication with strings upon strings attached should I dip further into this territory.

She squints into the sunlight as she searches the docks for Janu.

I don't think I'll be forgetting that kiss anytime soon. But it's enough to know I enjoyed it, and I am growing in my affection for her, but she is without a doubt too intricate for my life. Knowing Esme, wanting her this way, in this damnable emotional capacity, is dangerous for us. There is no passionate fling with Esme. She isn't that sort of woman and I don't tend to be that sort of man. Getting involved means really getting involved.

And I'm at a time in my life where I'm uncertain of where I'll go. What I'll be doing—if I decide to return to the Phantoms when this business with Esme is over, and that's a position I can't bring a woman into. It's not fair or right.

Especially not with one that belongs to Zach.

"You've got your angry face on, Dayton."

"Hmm?"

Esme is counting the coins in her hand. Janu is near enough I can hear his reggae rap from the boat.

"You look angry. I hope I didn't do anything else to tick you off today. I've been on my best behavior."

"Is that what you call today? Your best behavior?" I don't smile and I don't laugh. It's a miracle.

She drops the change into her pocket and sighs. "Sure. I think. It got rocky this morning, but I'm going to call that a draw, what with you having been the one to kiss me."

I'd like nothing better than to kiss her—now.

"But for the rest of the day, I have been considerate and let you play stupid. And I didn't make you come into the lingerie shop with me."

No one could have made me go in that place with Esme. I would have cut my own throat.

"First, the kiss, as we discussed, was a mistake and nothing else. Second, if you think you can make me go anywhere, then perhaps I should remind you of who I am and what I do."

"Right. You're an assassin."

"Yes. But just for the hell of it, let's keep that juicy tidbit to the confines of my home."

I stop in front of the skiff where Janu is flipping through his phone. There's grocery sacks and boxes at the stern. Good. We were running low on supplies and asked Janu to replenish.

I usually am the one to select groceries and supplies. I felt it necessary to keep Esme close.

Close enough, she didn't notice my continual scope of every corner and individual—no new faces or persons of interest. Even with the gun under my arm and the knife on my belt, I felt as I always do coming to Punta Cana. Safe and mildly overwhelmed.

"Good day?"

"Yes, thank you, Janu. Did you have any trouble?

He shakes his head, and accepts a wad of bills. His grin is gap-toothed revealing one gold cap, resembling a Hispanic pirate. I enjoy his company and prefer him to the other 'helpers' on the island. We understand one another best—how I prefer to keep things confidential. Mum is always the word between two criminals. There is no need to discuss why or complicate things the way a civilian might—like the woman at my side, tapping her foot.

"The water is good today. It will take only thirty minutes to return."

"Good."

I help Esme onto the boat and set her on a ripped leather seat. Her eyes skim over the gentle swells and then come back to mine when the boat buzzes away from the dock.

"Why don't you have your own boat?"

"Not reasonable with me gone most of the year."

She laughs. "And a huge mansion on a personal island is?"

"Priorities I guess."

"Zachariah tells me you don't have any family to go home to."

I do my best to be patient. Zach can tell whoever the hell he likes about my past. It matters little that Esme and I had a previous conversation on my lack of family.

"Yes. It's as we discussed before."

"I grew up in the foster system in America. I never had anybody until Zachariah.

The image of a lost little girl dropped from house to house makes me frown.

"I read that in your file. That's no way for a child to be raised. It must have been difficult."

"Yes. I hated moving. The different schools. Some families were nice, others—they weren't. It made you grow up fast. And in my case, I did some bad things when I was eighteen and got out on my own. I'm sure you read about it, but it's different talking about it. I guess it was my way of showing them all that I could do—that I no longer needed permission."

"I felt the same way. Only, when my old man was killed in a bar fight, the neighbor who took care of me wanted the monthly government checks, and favored a leather belt with his liquor. I was too young to do anything else until I turned seventeen and risked surviving on the streets. I was easy prey."

I am connected to Esme in a way I don't want to be. I offer a wry smile. "Well, we know how I ended up."

"Yeah, but I've actually been thinking about that."

"Have you now?"

The woman never stops thinking.

"Shopping isn't just for fun, it's therapeutic. It helps for thinking. Especially when you have an unwilling partner to do it with. But thinking about your—" She glances at Janu and lowers her voice, "your profession. I've decided, you never had a choice about your life. So you've made the best of it. And honestly, working for my father isn't the worst thing you could have done. Plus, like you said, you're a moral . . . man. So that's a good thing too."

My island is coming into view. The front windows gleam.

"I'm sorry, where are you going with this?"

She exhales, and folds her hands in her lap. "We have a lot in common."

I am tempted to laugh, but don't. Because she is serious.

"I wouldn't say that exactly."

Determination ripples in her gaze and makes me assess her with fresh eyes. She's working an angle I'm afraid I'm not going to like.

"We have my father in common. A rough background and a bad childhood. I . . . did something to a man. And you've done lots of somethings to . . . men. So, that gives us things in common."

I'm wondering if Esme spent too much time in the sun. Pray let that be it.

"Okay. We share a few things. I'll give you that."

"And . . ." Her eyes look up to mine. She blushes. "I

think we're interested in one another. Romantically speaking."

My stomach drops as I follow the little dots she drew. The dots I don't want to see.

"One kiss does not mean I'm interested romantically in you. It means I had a lapse in judgement. One that you would do well to forget."

"It does mean you are attracted to me."

I'm ready to argue but we know it won't work. Trying to remain calm, I forge on.

"Even if that is so, it doesn't mean what you think it ought to."

"And what do I think it ought to mean?" She asks, eyes deceptively innocent.

Where did this she-wolf come from? One day, a woman with scars and fears, today—only bold decisions in her eyes.

"You know damn well what you were hinting at. And I'm telling you it's a bad idea. We wouldn't be good for one another. You're at a bad place in your life and I'm transitioning!"

"True." She's looking down.

"And when you're done playing house with me, you've got a life and a job to go back to. So do I. And I also happen to work for your father. That should give you definite pause when you consider someone like me. I'm not interested in making any commitments. Of any kind."

"Yes. That's something to consider."

I suppose I don't hear her laugh because I'm too busy laying out my own arguments, and keep talking even though the boat is docking and Janu is grabbing a rope to tie in.

"Besides everything else I mentioned, I may be attracted, but I don't see you in that capacity. The one to which you are clearly referring."

I see her in every gosh-damn capacity.

Her eyes are dancing. "I see."

"Damn it, Esme. Stop doing that."

"Doing what?"

"Being so agreeable. I know you aren't listening to a damn thing I'm saying."

With a handful of bags she climbs off the boat.

I'm cursing. I bid Janu goodbye, and follow with armloads of food and clothes. By the time I reach the house I've worked up a whole different speech. Until I see Esme standing at my stove, going through my cabinets and picking through my groceries, as if she belongs there.

She looks like she does.

I panic. I don't need a woman disrupting my life. Especially not a woman who shares DNA with the man I consider a father.

"What time does Jacque get here? I'd like to help make the dinner tomorrow."

"What?" I try to change the focus from the collapse of my arguments to dinner and Jacque.

She pulls out a short vine of tomatoes, and has the audacity to smile. As if she didn't railroad me on the boat or leave things at loose ends. Twice in one day, the woman has me scrabbling around like a clown.

"Jacque. He is the man you said is coming to help with security?"

When I say nothing she continues.

"Anyways, I'd like to help you cook dinner. I've been meaning to ask you. I'd like to learn something about cooking. It always looks so delicious and pretty when you cook. Like a painting. I think it would be fun to learn."

"Wait . . . wait just one damn minute. Where do you get off bringing up a relationship between the two of us and then jumping over it like it's nothing?"

Esme drops the tomatoes on the counter. "I didn't bring up a relationship, you did. But I do think it would have been nice to consider."

"Would have been?"

She shrugs, irritating me with how easy and casual she's treating this, and sighs.

"Well, you gave plenty of good reasons why it isn't a good idea. I agree, those reasons are good. And if you don't see me that way, even if you are attracted to me and I to you, then I guess there is nothing else to discuss."

I might be tripping over myself in this conversation but I do not miss her challenge. Beneath the sweet drip of agreement, that derisive wolf is hiding. And I know exactly what it means. She thinks to play this off and make me fall into a trap? Then she's met the wrong man. Adding layers of sweetness to hide her true motives, doesn't mean I don't know what she's all about. Esme Costello has never played in the big leagues before. Not with a man like me.

"Right. I guess that's it."

Her eyes lighten. It's like trying to read the ocean. Unpredictable—and dangerous.

"I guess it is. Now, about those cooking lessons?"

"I could show you a few things, but not tonight."

My wariness shows through, because she laughs and comes around the kitchen island to stand closer to me. I expect her to pat my cheek.

"I promise not to bite you or anything. I simply want to learn."

I think she wants to do a hell of lot more than that, but I can't accuse the woman of doing anything when she's so—so . . . .

I stare at the groceries. If a petite little blond can intimidate me, then my boast of being in the big leagues, is only that. A boast.

"Good. I've got groceries to take care of. You should go put away your clothes. Or count your new shoes, or something."

She laughs as she leaves. "Or something."

When she's out of sight, I rip the fridge open and pop open a beer.
Women.

Chapter 8 *Murdering Sleep*

Esme

I can't move. He's going to kill me this time and no one will hear me scream for help. No one will even know what happened to me. I'll just be gone.

Carl's face, handsome and chiseled looms over me. His perfectly white capped teeth are bared in a grin, and my vision fades as air leaves.

All at once the pressure stops and I gasp in a precious mouthful of air.

Carl laughs. He laughs at me as I curl into a ball and sob into his expensive silk sheets. My voice is hoarse and broken. I can't tell if the alcohol is in control or if he is. But is there really a difference? Lately, he snaps at anything. Lately, all he seems to enjoy is hurting me.

"God you're beautiful."

I squirm violently when he reaches for me and rolls me under him. His weight is heavy on my stomach, his hands sweaty as they paw my breasts and neck, touching the bruises he caused, tracing them with reverence. His speech is slurred and I close my eyes to block him out. I can feel darkness, but not the sort that comes from having the life choked out of you. It's beckoning.

There is a gun between the box spring and the mattress. I've seen Carl check its position, seen him load it, and clean it. He has several, but this one always stays in the mattress. And I can reach it if I try hard enough.

I could make it all end. I could stop him.

I've tried leaving. Tried hiding from him. He always finds me.

I stopped loving Carl a very long time ago. And now, I feel nothing toward him. Except fear. But to take his life?

He leans forward, kisses me sloppily, runs his hands down my stomach and sighs with pleasure. How soon before he accidently kills me? Before he chokes too hard or hits me one too many times?

Molin won't help me. No one will. I'm alone.

I hold my tears, and force my breaths to even so Carl won't hear it.

"You like it, don't you baby?"

I shake my head. "Please Carl."

His hands circle my neck, to play at the tendons where my pulse beats erratically.

"Shut up."

I snap my mouth closed and go rigid when his grip returns to my throat, when his hands sink deep into the flesh and my air is cut off. Staring up into wide black eyes, I see nothing in them. They are as vacant as Carl's soul.

I don't think about what I do. Or why. I already know this is the way it ends between us. But in these precious seconds, I don't hesitate, I don't stop, not until my left hand closes over the cold grip and my finger is on the trigger.

The explosion is earth shattering.

I wake up screaming.

There's blood all over me. I can see it. On my hands and face, in my hair. It's sticky and wet. I'll never get it off. Near retching, I tumble out of my sheets slicked with sweat and make it to the bathroom. Terror pulls at my insides. My hands are trembling as I switch on the lights.

There's nothing. Where I felt sticky red, there is only pale skin. I stare for several seconds the tears track my face and I do the one thing Carl tried to steal from me—I breathe.

It is too real.

I shudder and I lean on the counter.

It's over.

And I killed him. I killed Carl and his heavy body fell on top of me. The blood was everywhere and knowing what I did sits like a ballast—even now—beneath my breastbone.

It had to be done. Didn't it? There was no other way.

I wouldn't change it. I would squeeze the trigger and repeat it all . . . it had to happen. Because Carl wasn't a man, he was a monster and if he didn't succeed in killing me, he would have gone on to some other plaything and done the same. He would hurt more women.

Hunched over the sink, I splash handfuls of water on my face. The cold is rejuvenating, and the nightmare recedes.

From the garden, a hint of roses and baby's breath floats in through the open windows. I breathe in the smell, close my eyes and picture the flowers—their dewy petals fluttering in the breeze, and their faces upturned for sun— or as they are now, gently closed to protect a tiny fairy within. The whimsical image is what I need to draw me out of the darkness I've fallen into.

I am safe. Dayton is near.

Rolling my neck, I step closer to the window, inhale deeply. A stroll in the moonlight, and the flowers, will do me good. It will settle my nerves.

In the kitchen, I pour a tall glass of merlot to help the garden do its work. It is only right to be helpful. I take the stairs to the pool level. The open expanse of windows makes it appear there is no barrier between the house and sea. The sight pairs nicely with my wine.

I walk the cobblestone path to the garden. I am not disappointed. The arbor is draped in blossoms and decorated in tiny white lights—like lightning bugs dancing. Even here Dayton has taken care to pay attention to details.

He likes the details, and rules—and everything to be in tidy boxes. A sentiment I understand completely. But can't fully adopt as my life has been so out of order and tossed around.

I take a mouthful of wine. I sing a hopeful tune from Cinderella.

"A dream, is a wish, your heart makes . . . ." I sigh, and sit on a bench beneath the arbor. "When you're fast asleep . . . ." The scent of roses is strong enough to make the tears come back.

To be honest, I might wish to never leave this place.

Maybe I'd spend my days tending a garden, cooking lavish meals, and swimming in the mild Caribbean seas. I could work from home for Magnifique. I am good at my job, with delegating, and if needed, I could fly out for short appearances to be assured of a project's performance. It will all work out swimmingly.

I laugh, finish off the wine and enjoy the buzz. I'm warm from the inside out, and it feels pretty damn good.

The only thing missing is the presence of a Dutchman who wishes he did not enjoy my company—as much as I enjoy his.

A hand clamps over my mouth.

Startled, I take too long to recognize it's a man's hand, and by the strong smell of aftershave, it is not Dayton. He drags me off the bench like a ragdoll, pinning me to him, one hand clamped on my mouth, the other around my stomach, and pulls me backward. I kick out, swinging my legs like a child throwing a tantrum. He grunts at the sudden shift of weight, but doesn't loosen. He speeds up, hurling us over brambles and rocks in his hurry to the water. My instinct to survive overrides the terror. I flail my legs, I claw with my nails, using every ounce of my weight to sink my butt to the ground.

It gets a response.

He stumbles over a rock, his hand slips and I scream. It shatters the air like a hammer smashing glass. He ignores it and walks faster.

The waves are crashing on the beach and I realize I can drown. Fear kicks me in the gut, and I have to fight to not weep. Where is my strength when I need it? Where is the courage I've been drawing on these past days for Dayton?

Fight for your life, Esme.

The water laps at my heels and we stop. He murmurs something that makes the hair on my arms stand on end. It's in Dutch. I can't make him out, but I don't have to be a genius to know this man works for the Torminas. No other family could find an off-the-grid island and then attempt to kill me.

I hope it's an attempt.

I'm lax. The man hefts me up easily, his hand slips again, and I scream with all my strength. Nothing stirs in response.

I cry. I land hard as a stone. I'm in a boat. A new horror floods me. They are kidnapping me so they can torture me first. That bastard Molin will probably finish me personally, because I killed his son.

The motor grinds, waves rock the boat.

A distinct crack rends the air.

The man beside me slumps.

My eyes jerk to the house and instead of Dayton

rushing to rescue me, a terrifying black wraith is snaking to the boat. My first captor guns the engine, another crack comes —sharper and louder, and I'm staring into the open, dead eyes of my kidnapper. Black dots on white saucers. I am in the hull, near paralyzed, as shock envelopes me. I'm stunned in revulsion as the boat lulls to a stop, still close to shore.

Trembling, I try to stand, to get out so I can get away from the bodies. My legs won't hold my weight with the sea beneath. Repeatedly, I collapse. I slosh about in a layer of wet I pray is only water. Hysteria grows with each attempt and by my fourth time, I'm sobbing.

The wraith is here. Dressed in black from head to toe, face like iron . . . with vivid green eyes. He jerks me from the watery grave. I don't complain about the rough handling, because I can't make my mouth work.

All I can do is chatter, sob and curl into the safety of Dayton's arms.

I'm thankful he doesn't try to push me away. Instead, he leaves the boat, and walks toward the house at a brisk pace. My eyes close. Suddenly I'm so tired I sink into Dayton. His arms are a protective cage, and his heart, is steady and sure beneath my ear and I let it center me. The cadence of life reminds me, I'm not dead. Somehow, I have escaped once more.

When we get inside, Dayton carries me to the second floor to a large bedroom. He deposits me onto the unmade bed and goes to a small wet bar.

My stomach rolls and I press my hand to my forehead to ebb this headache, or quell the urge to vacate my stomach on Dayton's carpet. I'm shaking, face wet with tears. And this sign of weakness makes me feel small and senseless in front of him.

He joins me at the foot of the bed and hands me a tumbler with whiskey. I accept the glass but stare into the amber liquid.

"Drink it."

I'm too weak to fight him. The liquid—like fire— tastes like nail polish remover. I cough, my eyes water, but I down another sip.

"Happy?" My voice is raspy.

"No. No, Esme I am not happy."

I shrink deeper into the mattress as if to hide and I have to stop myself from melting into the comforter for a place to cower. I can't handle Dayton's anger tonight. Not now.

"You left the house."

"Yes," I whisper, pressing my lips together to avoid sobbing. *And nearly killed for it.*

"And you didn't tell me."

I search for the strong part of me I regained these last months. I don't want to be this frightened little waif. I'm not that woman. No longer. I'm not.

With the help of the whiskey, I form a complete sentence. "It's the middle of the night. I only wanted to sit in the garden."

His eyes reflect the violence of the evening. His stare is cold and brutal. He killed men for me. I'm grateful.

"How could you have been so stupid?"

Startled by Dayton's anger, I am no longer at the point of crumbling. The desire to fight is growing stronger by the second.

"I was tired! I wasn't thinking!

"Exactly."

I fumble to my feet and poke him hard.

"I didn't just almost get killed to piss you off. Stop yelling at me. I can't handle it right now."

"I'm not the one who nearly got drug off my island. You could have been killed on the spot. I could have been too late. Do you understand that, Esme? I barely managed to save you." His face reddens.

The last words are said with such emotion, I

struggle to hide my tears. In Dayton's eyes, in the unyielding bite of his voice, is real concern—even fear for me. Have I ever experienced real concern over my welfare until now? I don't think so. It calms everything in me and tempers my desire to claw him.

"I do, Dayton. Please, stop talking to me like I'm a child. I needed some air and I wasn't thinking about my safety."

His jaw sets and I cross my arms, fighting tears. "I had some nightmares. I got a glass of wine and went to the garden. It was stupid. I know that now. You don't need to hammer it into me."

Dayton draws nearer to me, body rigid. Something in this Dayton is different. Something I want to hold close, for fear of it leaving.

"Dayton holds my chin and looks into me. You scared the hell out of me, Esme."

All I can think of to say is, "I'm sorry."

His eyes are softer than I've ever seen them. He drops his hand from my face.

"I know."

"Thank you."

"Don't thank me. I should have been more careful with you."

I'm feeling steady now, although my limbs are heavy. I want to lay down, and forget this night ever happened. Preferably with Dayton at my side.

"It's my fault. Not yours. Please don't blame yourself. I brought this madness here."

"They would have tried to come in. Those men didn't come all this way to hide out in the bushes, Esme. They came for you. My guess is to take you to their boss."

I agree with him. It doesn't sit well with the whiskey.

"Will we have to leave the island?" My eyes want to close.

Dayton ignores my question, instead, reaches for my hand with a curse black enough to make me blush.

"What did you do to your hands?"

There are streaks of blood and scrapes on my palms and fingers.

"Trying to escape . . . it's just a few scratches."

"Stay here."

"Why?"

I lean back on the bed. The sheets are thrown to the side. I've never been in Dayton's room. Let alone his floor of the house. I feel like an invader. My hands are at my sides. My eyes are like ten pound weights. I could sleep sitting up at this point.

The sting of antiseptic jolts me upright, and I gasp as Dayton pulls my hand into his lap.

"Hold still.

"I don't need you to doctor me. I need to sleep."

He looks up from the cotton ball with frigid eyes. I let him finish, but comfort myself in the knowledge I'm too weak to argue. I close my eyes and the heat of his rough hands on mine lulls me back toward sleep. He lingers every few minutes, and I'm fairly certain it's to check my pulse. I savor every moment.

Dayton finishes and orders me to get some sleep, I don't even protest that I'm not in my bed. Mostly because Dayton is already plopping me beneath his comforter, and dimming the lights.

My last recollection is Dayton standing at the doorway to his room, a tall silhouette.

Chapter 9 *Man of Action*

Dayton

Esme sleeps for twelve hours. And I don't close my eyes for a second of it.

Standing in front of the video monitors for the island, I finish off my fifth cup of coffee. I rub the five o'clock shadow I'm sporting. I've gone over the footage of the previous night several times, and in each frame, my anger reaches a new level.

They came to my island—my island, and nearly got away with Zach's daughter because of my incompetence . . . with Esme. The acid from hours of caffeine-overloading broils up. I've been at this long enough the screens are blurring.

I step back from the computers, check to see if the barrier fences are up and running, and close the door to the security room. Outside, the sun is bright and I'm reminded life does exist outside of that room.

It is by the grace of God I woke to the sound of Esme screaming. I tore back my covers and charged down the steps, ready to defend. But when I reached Esme's door, I could hear her in the bathroom, the water running, and her crying. The screaming apparently was a nightmare. I wanted to open the door and comfort her, but I didn't.

Perhaps it was cowardice, or fear of deepening the bond between us if I found Esme crying. Either way, I gave her privacy.

I didn't hear the perimeter alarms until twenty minutes later.

It was almost too late. I made it in time to see a man dragging Esme into the boat. I acted strictly on emotion.

I never have before.

Even now, the fear and rage flash in my mind. Constant and infuriating.

I ignore my first impulse to head to the second floor where I know Esme is sleeping, and instead go straight to the gym. I flip on the switches, and head for the weights and my stereo. I crank Five Finger Death Punch to an ear bleeding volume and work through my reps without stopping. Iron and muscle-burn is a welcome respite this morning and I use the sweat and fire to chip away at my anger that felt insurmountable a few hours ago.

Half an hour in, I switch from weights to treadmill and program an incline with speed.

It's punishment, but I need my mind to filter into this emotional dead zone. In this place, I can think clearly, and work efficiently.

I've had my suspicions since the beginning of this. There are only a handful of families large enough, with a reach in the European circuit to accomplish an attack on my island.

Useless endeavor or not, I spent three hours driving the boat out deep, weighting the bodies and returning to hide the skiff in the reeds of the far east barrier.

I have a two-mile wedge of land to myself. One I foolishly thought to keep pure and unsoiled in regard to my career. I am disappointed not having met that goal. And relieved at having already planned out areas in which to dispose bodies.

Once a hitman, always a hitman. Or something

along those lines.

Nearing the five-mile mark, there's a sizzle in my bones and I bump up the speed in this last mile.

Zachariah kept Molin from me. I can pray he has done this as a way to protect me, yet it does little in the way of comfort. It does the opposite. Rage vibrates in me, followed by a sense of betrayal.

I've been lied to, kept in the dark, and cheated before. But I never expected it to come from Zachariah Moncleve.

I mull it over, wishing I'm wrong and coming to the same conclusion I did this morning at four. If my suspicions were not enough, there is no possibility I could have missed the mark of a condor on the forearms of the corpses. A mark I once hoped to bear, after I had been properly initiated. One I never gained, courtesy of Zach. I would have worn it like a brand—and been taken to slaughter when I became less useful.

And I wanted desperately to be one of them. Anything to get out on my own. Regardless the cost.

What I gained was one mistake after another, until they sent me on a suicide mission to assassinate Zachariah Moncleve. It took me several years to reconcile with the idea that Molin Tormina sent me to die. He didn't care whether I succeeded or not, he likely hoped I'd be killed and taken off his hands. Nineteen years old and I had already outgrown my usefulness.

At the time, I was too naïve to realize the depth of darkness I stumbled into, or what the cost of living in that darkness might be.

I stop the treadmill and step off—with rubber legs. I knew, all along the Tormina family would come back to haunt me, and Zach would only hide something like this from me, if they had. But that doesn't change my current predicament. Or the bitter taste of wrongdoing in my mouth.

I need answers.

And I'm not going to get them on my island, ignoring the obvious. I've got to return to Phantom headquarters.

Spain is lovely this time of year and I'm long overdue for a visit. Thinking of the Mediterranean villa on the hills of Madrid makes me grin. I think it fair not to warn Zach of our impending arrival, but I regret Jacque will reach the island too late to see us leave. He won't take it personally, as he never does anything. I've been dancing around this conclusion all night, when I've known all along what has to be done.

Any safety I enjoyed by the exclusivity of my island is lost. For now, the Dominican Republic is not a home I can return to. And I have to get Esme as far from here as possible—as quickly as I can. The kills have a ripple effect, and news will reach Molin by the end of the day, if it hasn't already. He is expecting a report.

Mind made up, I head in the direction of the kitchen. Esme is sitting at the bar, sipping coffee. It's a small blessing I didn't have to see her in my bed before rousing her.

The smell of the brew makes my stomach shrivel. I have to pass. I don't say anything until I've uncapped a bottle of water and downed half. But my eyes are flowing over her, checking and rechecking. There are shadows beneath her eyes.

"Sleep well?"

"Yes. You shouldn't have let me sleep so long."

"You needed it. It was a rough night." Her eyes travel the length of me then stop on my face. I'm not the only one checking.

"Looks like it was a rougher one for you. Did you sleep at all?"

I stroke my bristled chin and smile. Wearing the sweat from the gym combined with my own set of dark circles, I'm sure I could succeed in frightening mothers with small children.

"I'll be better when I get cleaned up. And eat something. You hungry?"

"I guess so."

"I'm going to make omelets with ham and cheese. Traditional but hearty."

"You killed two men last night."

I close the refrigerator. My stomach jumps at the subtle judgement in her tone.

"Yes. It was that or watch you be sailed off into the night. Would you prefer I didn't?"

"No."

"Then what? You prefer I mope about? Feeling terrible for doing it?" I crack six eggs into the skillet, refusing to give her full eye contact. I glance over my shoulder at her pale face. She looks just shy of broken. Her hair is messy. She holds a mug. I wish I could be the man to fix her.

"I'm not that sort of man. I've killed too many times to be. So don't ask or expect it, Esme."

I think I've done a damn good job at shoving her away from me—again. It's for the best. As I finish cooking, her voice destroys the silence.

"You never answered me last night about having to leave the island."

I plate the omelets and garnish them with watercress. I'm comfortable in the kitchen. Ten years ago, I would have laughed at the thought of cooking above the level of a frozen waffle.

A different man, a different lifetime.

"I hadn't decided what I wanted to do yet."

"And you have now?" She braces, hands folded in front of her.

"Yes. We leave as soon as you're packed. I've already booked us flights from Punta Cana to Madrid."

Esme stares, her eyes rounding. "Spain? To my father?"

"That is exactly where we are going. Now, I'd like some answers, Esme."

"But I can't talk about—"

I stop her. My blood is rising close to boiling. I don't need a reminder of Zach's betrayal and I certainly don't want to punish a woman who isn't responsible for it. She did what her father told her to do—what I might have told her, were the situations reversed. But they aren't.

"I already know you are involved with the Tormina family." I try to speak softly. "And now I'd like you to explain how. I can't work with my hands tied."

Any argument she might have had, appears to drain from her, as well as her color. I regret only that Esme has gotten herself involved with Molin at all. The man is a viper. He would sooner gut then offer assistance in a crisis. It draws another connection between us I prefer never existed.

Esme watches me, guarded, weary, but I know she's strong. I hope that strength will carry her forward.

"I killed Carl."

"Carl Tormina?" The wretched son of a bitch who took a disliking to me upon my first introduction to Molin.

"Yes." Her voice has dropped to a whisper.

I squeeze her hand.

"I killed him."

I have no doubt the man deserved it. But hearing and seeing this woman admit killing when she is as frail as a moth in my hands, doesn't compute well. If possible, the urgency to protect her, grows stronger.

"You protected yourself."

Esme jerks, her nostrils flaring as she regards me with what can only be described as dismay. "How can you say that? You don't even know what happened."

"I don't need to know." I release Esme's hand and

touch a finger to her cheek where a tear escaped. It might as well have slid down my heart.

"You are good. That's all I need to know. All I care about."

I expect her to bristle, or be surprised at the gentleness in my voice and the emotion threaded into it, but she surprises me by pressing my hand to her cheek. In this breath between us, I can imagine growing old with such a face. I can imagine giving everything I have in order to keep it. Those exact dangerous feelings must be quashed.

"Thank you for helping me last night."

"I did only what was necessary." My thoughts are warring for control over one another, "Not true. You helped me. You cared for me."

Esme's breath warms me. We are too close.

She sees me, and is looking in places too dark for her. I draw back, severing the contact and inhale to dispel my tremor. "I need to get cleaned up. And you have some packing to do."

"Dayton, please don't pull away from me."

"There is nothing between us to pull away from. I have things to do. And so do you."

I leave, even though her expression crumples. When I ought to be congratulating myself for a job well done—I feel like the worst of heels.

Chapter 10 *No Habla Español*

Esme

Madrid is like I expected. Only older and far more ornate than any postcard or movie could do justice. The vitality of history is breathtaking. I picture conquistadors on destriers for gold and glory, or the violent show of man versus beast in the running of the bulls. Both images easily fit amidst the shopping centers, tourist attractions, and overpriced 'authentic' Spanish food. It's all I can do to take it in without being overwhelmed by the diversity of this city.

The stream of movement from the window of our taxi makes my insides tremble in anticipation—then fear.

I met my father once before. In a coffee shop, two blocks from the Magnifique lobby. He came to Amsterdam hoping to kindle a relationship with me. I offered him a pen pal instead. Of course, over the last two years, our relationship has morphed into occasional phone calls and a whopping total of two video chats. Now, I'm coming to him with unprecedented conditions. Once again, I am running to my father hoping he can shield me from my mistakes.

Sitting beside Dayton as the cab races through the streets makes me want to break into hysterics—not the kind that results in female blubbering but the kind likened to the

Joker whilst cackling over a bomb of nerve gas. Neither Dayton nor the driver would think me sane if I gave into my base impulses. But it's tempting.

We drive past a festive piazza strung with multicolor prayer flags, hordes of fountains and countless churches with mother Mary perched above arched doorways. We don't slow until we get to a place that is above Madrid's throbbing center. Here, the wind is marked with saffron and paprika. It smells like an *abuela's* kitchen and it makes me wonder who my *abuelita* might be. I have never been brave enough with my father to ask about his own family. We haven't gone that deep yet.

Dayton is completely at ease as he watches the landscape change. We've hardly spoken since leaving the island.

"It's a little awe-inspiring to see Spain for the first time."

"Yes. It's beautiful."

"They say the sunsets of Madrid and Barcelona are the best in the world."

"You'll see for yourself tonight."

I can't imagine a waning sun makes this painting of the city look any better than it already does.

"Does he know we're coming?"

Dayton's smile is the one I recognize as amused with a touch of cynicism.

"He will very soon. We're close."

Such words have never been sweeter. After hours of never-ending flights and waiting, I don't think I've ever been so desperate for a bed. No matter that the only thing keeping me awake are my nerves, which are currently squabbling in my stomach. After the worst is over, I'm sure I can sleep for days. Make that months. And when I wake up, this nightmare will be over.

We pull up in front of an alabaster mansion, my mouth drops open and my fear takes a backseat.

Architecturally, the building is stunning . . . sculpted.

Arches, large pillars, and never ending white marble make the house appear not only larger than life but Greek in style. I step out before the driver can assist me, and stare at gargoyles and angels playing out a war between the roof and steps. I've never seen such a thing and it's very fitting, considering what my father does for a living.

Silently, Dayton urges me on. I've completely forgotten my bags. I glance back and see Dayton, however unfriendly these last hours, is ever the gentleman and is carrying my duffle for me. I want to protest for the sake of arguing that the fairer sex is in need of no handouts. I decide not to.

Like strangers needing a place to rest for the night, we walk straight up to the massive double gold filigree doors and press the intercom button. Or rather, Dayton does. I am struck with paralyzing anxiety, and cannot speak. I'm too busy gawking at the 14 karat on the front door to notice when they burst inward.

Standing in the open doorway, wearing a silk shirt, open at the collar, with a gold chain and crucifix, is the man I forgot is so handsome. My father.

"Saints, Dayton, not even a phone call? *Mon Dieu*!"

"I didn't think it necessary . . . considering."

"No, of course. I can see you have some things you wish to discuss with me."

Zach's eyes, nothing like my own, are dark and flare with his own anger as he assesses us.

"*Oui*." Dayton answers in a tone that is polite and unrepentant, and breezes by my father without another word. I follow him in as Zachariah closes the door. The entryway is awe-inspiring.

Smiling, I awkwardly accept Zachariah's warm embrace and French double kiss, then stand like a lame goat by an elaborate bench beneath an outrageous wall mirror as he looks me up and down with the distinct note of disapproval in his eyes. I'm proud I do not squirm under his scrutiny but rather accomplish a detached expression raising my head.

"*Elle est trop fatiguée. Trop mince. Qu'avez-vous fait à ma fille?*" This question is not for me, but rather my silent companion.

Dayton moves so quickly I stumble back. His eyes are filled with restrained anger. Apparently they are no longer going to remain civil. "*J'ai gardé sa vie. Qui est plus que vous semblez être capable de faire sur votre proper!*"

I work to recall my French. They are already squaring up for battle . . . in this expensive entryway? It doesn't seem like proper grounds for a duel.

"*Vous avez menti pour moi.*"

"*J'ai été qui vous protège.*"

I've had enough of being left out of the conversation. I step between them, risking life and limb by the expression in Dayton's eyes. My father is more on edge than I've ever seen him.

"English, please. Not French. Not when I know you are arguing about me. At least partially. Now isn't the time to be fighting."

Zachariah throws his hands into the air. "He is angry that I lied to him."

"You did keep Tormina from him." I add.

The men's eyes jump to me and I get out of the line of fire.

"Whatever you both said—I'm fairly certain there was something in there about me being too thin and not well rested—there are greater things here to discuss. Like, for example, why we are here in the first place."

With obvious concern, Zach asks Dayton. "What has happened?"

Dayton's shoulders fall and his sigh sounds of exhaustion. The worst is over.

"Less than forty-eight hours ago, two of Tormina's men came to the island and tried to take Esme. It was dealt with."

His face hardens. I try not to fidget when my father's eyes are back on me, filled with fury.

"And you are fine, *oui*? No injuries?"

"None. Not even a scratch." Not entirely true. But I don't need to interject that particular tidbit. The tension is thick enough to drown in.

"Forgive me Esme. You must be exhausted. *Je suis tellement désolé.*"

"It's been a long trip."

"*Oui*, I will have Adrienne show you to the guest room while I speak with Dayton. I can see there is much to discuss." His hands are tense at his sides.

I feel a breaking between the men—which I have no place in. Accepting this, I am relieved I might get a chance to close my eyes before doing anything else. A few seconds later, a woman pops in. She addresses my father first, in French, then looks at me when he speaks English. Undoubtedly for my sake, as Dayton is fluent in French.

"Adrienne, please take my daughter to the west wing for a suitable room. Perhaps the one with the best view? And call Dimitri. We'll eat early this evening."

With wide hips, a narrow waist, and large brown eyes, Adrienne would be better suited to a skin-tight leopard-print dress rather than the plain black maid's uniform. I sense a few 'vibes' between my father and the maid before we part and head in the direction of stairs. I allow only a minute of worry over Dayton and my father. The two will mend fences.

"No elevator?" I hope to lighten the mood.

Adrienne's smile puts me immediately at ease. "No. I've been telling your father he should install one. There are four floors. It can be so tiring moving up and down the levels throughout the day."

"How many wings are there?"

"East and west. Family quarters are on the third and fourth floors in the west wing. Servant quarters are in the east of the upper floors. The lower two floors are utilized for your father's work."

I stop on a landing, in shock, at an exceptional print by Salvador Dali, framed in ebony. As far as I know, the original is locked away safe in some museum.

"Is this The Burning Giraffe?"

Adrienne seems pleased with me and nods. "Yes, it is one of your father's favorites. He likes the strange and Salvador Dali is certainly an acquired taste. He commissioned the copy some years back."

"Surrealism is one of those things you either love or you hate."

"And you like it?"

I smile. "It's different. But captivating. You don't see bodies with drawers built into them beside a flaming giraffe every day."

"No." Adrienne grins. Silver glints in her hair. It makes her smooth complexion younger with the contradiction of age in her mahogany hair.

When we reach the top of the stairs, I sigh. It shouldn't matter who my father might show an interest in romantically or not, but I don't stop myself from asking. I have to know if this pretty woman wearing plain black is important to him. Maybe because I've been starved for female companionship or maybe because I want to pass the level of pen pal with my father. Nearly killed and being on the run for your life, puts things into perspective.

"Can I ask if you and Zachariah are . . . together?"

Adrienne raises her eyebrows before speaking. "I suppose I should wait to confirm what is between us until your father has a chance to explain."

I don't flinch.

"But I won't. We have been eloped for the last five years. He would prefer to be formally married, but my family wouldn't have permitted a marriage to a foreigner, let alone Moncleve."

"But . . . you sound French."

"I am named after my great-grandmother, a wonderful French woman. But my family primarily hails from Spain."

I follow Adrienne through the long corridor of the fourth floor. "Don't take this the wrong way, but you don't sound Spanish. I mean, your coloring looks it and you're beautiful, but I don't hear it."

Adrienne's laughter fills the hall. The woman has a way about her. Something so vibrant she reminds me of the city of Madrid at first sight. Overwhelming and beautiful. I'm happy for my father for finding her. And happy too, that it's easy to relax with her.

"That is very kind of you. I'll have to tell Zachariah. But no, my accent became muddled when I was sent to boarding school in France for my adolescent years."

"Is that where you met my father?"

"Oh no. We met years later. I finished with schooling at the age of twenty-three. I didn't meet your father for another ten years. A pity, but when the time was right, it was right."

I try to estimate her age. I suppose I'm too tired for even simple arithmetic . . . but I've also never been good at mental math. My intended question falls flat as Adrienne opens the door to the last room at the end of the hall. I am suddenly transported to a Parisian villa. Outfitted in crème, gold, and pale pink, I am instantly tempted to bum rush the bed and flop face first into the silk bedspread.

"Wonderful, isn't it?"

The ceiling is covered in pale cherubim with fluffy white clouds. "It's a masterpiece. Like walking into a Paris crème puff."

"I told your father something of the same."

He considered every detail, including putting late forties style perfume bottles and gilded mirrors on the dresser with a soft backed chair set in front of a large lace dressing screen. I'm in hog heaven. Woman heaven.

"I'll let you have some time to get settled. Supper won't be for a few hours and the men will need some time to go over things."

I stop her. "Adrienne, it's lovely to meet you."

She smiles, walks over to me and presses one short kiss to each of my cheeks. "And even lovelier to meet you. I never thought to have children, but you make a lovely daughter."

Chapter 11 *The Truce Will Set You Free*

Dayton

The majority of my anger lessened within moments of seeing him and has dwindled in the long walk to a room I am as familiar with as my home on the island—his study. Designed like The Oval Office, in the year since I've been in Spain nothing has changed. His desk is cluttered with paperwork, his laptop open and running a program amid a hoard of uncapped pens and two empty glasses.

Zach has positioned himself by the massive curved windows, a smoking cigar leaning on an ashtray. His back is to me but I sense he is waiting for me to speak.

"You'll never change."

"Not likely." Zach turns, smiling. "I'm sorry for not telling you of the Tormina family, Dayton"

That's good to hear.

"Thank you for apologizing."

"But?"

I shuffle some of the papers on his desk to keep from stuffing my hands into my pockets. Twelve years have not impacted how I view myself with Zach. Whether it be a father figure, or the leader of a multibillion-dollar assassin corporation, I doubt I will ever feel on the same level as that man.

Even now, knowing I've killed more men than him—I stand several inches taller, and I feel like I'm nineteen—young, impressionable, and desperate for acceptance. But I am not that person anymore.

"Why? Why keep it a secret when you know I've been wanting to settle a score?"

"That is exactly why I kept it from you. You have a temper. And a penchant for trouble when the time calls for it. I didn't want you getting involved again with the Torminas. In any way."

I know he isn't finished, and I give him the courtesy of explaining before I tear into him.

"Dayton, over the years our relationship has become familial. You work for me, yes, but in all the ways that count, you are a son to me."

Zach's disarming smile, the one that first got beneath my guard by the docks years ago, makes me pause.

"A beloved son, and I didn't want to risk you. In any way."

I want to rail against his words, but I accept them. The Torminas will always be a sore spot for me and as much as Zach wanted to protect me, he took this chance away from me.

"I'm your best operative."

"*Oui!* But you and I know you don't enjoy it. This was never meant to be . . . it, for you. You know this. I know it. And we know killing comes at a price. Killing with emotion—is never a good choice."

"I don't need a babysitter, Zach."

"No, you need someone to remind you of who you are. And what you want. If I had told you about the Tormina family, what would you have done, hmm?"

"I would have killed them. Systematically eradicated the family and any who might think to retaliate. It's a big job, but I could have gotten help. Jacque's an excellent shot."

Zach's mouth twitches. "You would kill Molin Tormina? Just like that? No second thoughts?

I hesitate, then curse. "I don't know."

"My exact concern for you. The Torminas need to be taken care of and I didn't want you to be involved . . . with the chance you may not be able to pull the trigger, or worse, you do and then regret your decision. He meant something to you Dayton—even if you don't want him to."

I didn't want to think about this. Not here, not ever.

"He meant nothing to me. He wanted me dead."

"Yes. But you can't lie to yourself or to me and say he didn't mean anything. You were young and he was your mentor."

"God, Zach, I should have stayed on my island."

"Well, I suppose I should apologize for that as well. I sent Esme to you."

I scowl at Zach, but can't help laugh. "You ambushed me."

"It was the only way. You're stubborn."

"Private and self-centered."

"That too."

I laugh out loud. My muscles are loosening, the tension I walked in with is gone.

"I've missed you, old man."

"I'm not old. I am perfectly aged. And I've missed you as well." Zach's s eyes shine with renewed mischief. "Might we like each other then?"

I sit on the edge of his desk and pick up his cigar. "Yes . . . Cuban?"

"Oh yes . . . and aside from the attack, how are you and Esme getting along?"

I inhale a mouthful of sweet smoke and pass the cigar to him. "Well enough." He can't know about the kiss . . . unless Esme called him the same night.

"Did she like the island . . . enjoy all the quiet?"

My instincts have kicked in. "She liked the island fine. Though I may have been boring. I wasn't particularly good company."

"Of course not." Zach puffs on the cigar and hands it back. "But I didn't think she wanted any for a while after what happened with Carl."

"She's a strong woman."

"Mmmm, that she is. She takes after her mother. Big blue eyes and blond hair. Looks very American."

"Acts very American too. Not a day has gone by where Esme isn't talking my ear off or asking me a question."

"I like a woman who can carry on a conversation, don't you?"

"Of course, but Esme has a way of agitating a man into wanting nothing but silence. And when that happens, it's . . . why are you smiling at me?"

"Is it wrong to be happy for you?"

"Happy for me?"

Zach laughs. "Dayton, for such a smart man, you are slow in the heart. Or has it escaped you how much you've taken to Esme . . . and she to you? I couldn't have planned a better match."

"What the hell are you talking about?"

"Am I wrong in thinking you are interested in Esme?"

"Yes, you're wrong. There's nothing between us."

"I see."

He doesn't see. Not at all. And I can tell by the glint in his eyes he thinks his plans are working out. Heat creeps up my neck, but I tamp it with cool annoyance. He cannot know how damn close to the mark he is.

"Did you think dumping your daughter—one which I had no knowledge of, by the way, on my island would foster some sort of—of relationship between us?"

"I hoped it might, yes. But apparently, I am

mistaken. No harm, no foul. *Oui*? *Mon erreur.*"

"Yes, your mistake. Damn it, Zach."

"I'm a Frenchman at heart. Do you blame me for wanting you to be happy? Or wanting grandchildren? I am aging."

I roll my eyes, taking in the lean and ageless figure. "Zachariah, you have three gray hairs, a babe for a woman who's ten years your junior and a house the size of a small country. You have everything you could ever need. Leave the matchmaking to the professionals."

"Ah well, you can't blame a man for trying. So! Are you hungry?"

I laugh, and wrap my arms around Zach in a bear hug. "Thank God, you're still you."

Several hours later, after wine, snow crab and pilaf, our little party is seated beneath a blanket of stars and freshly cleaned glass in a massive observatory. From the outside, a family enjoying some quality time together, from within, we discuss battle tactics and exchange information on the Tormina family.

"The stronghold will be in Amsterdam and I've no doubt that's where Molin will have scurried off to when he hears of our leaving the island unharmed."

Esme and I share a look.

"Who do you have running the job?"

Zach drapes his arm over Adrienne's shoulders and sighs. "I assigned Benson as point then added Jacque as co-leader. They've assembled their own team. Four in total. The last weeks have been spent researching on where, when and how best to accomplish the task with as much privacy as possible. We don't want to create a media scandal. Not only would that go over poorly for the Phantom's reputation, but it would risk outing Esme as a connection."

I can sense Esme tense. "You are talking about killing an entire family."

"Yes. It's what we do for a living. And this family has been a blight since their origin. Now they need taking care of. Or do you want to look over your shoulder for the rest of your life? After of course, you've changed your hair color, eye color, and identity."

"I'm sorry my darling, but Dayton is correct. I know it must seem strange to speak of death so callously, but my organization kills with the utmost discrimination. What we deem appropriate to fill a contract is passable for capital punishment in most countries. These men are evil to their core. Make no mistake they kill without a thought."

"I know this already. This entire thing is frightening. Talking about killing people, planning how to do it quietly, wondering if they'll make another attempt to get me. I don't like it."

"Nor should you." Zach stands and places his hand on Esme's shoulder.

I'm jealous of the contact.

"I'm sorry if it's come too much too soon. We were insensitive. In the future I will discuss business without you."

She stands and crosses her arms.

"No, that isn't what I want. I don't want to be treated like an invalid. I already feel helpless. I want to learn."

"Learn the business?" Zach says with surprise.

"Yes. And I want to learn how to defend myself. I don't want to be at the mercy of whoever might be able to help. I want to stop them myself."

"That will not ever happen again. This building is one of the safest in the world."

"Zach, she has a point. I could have been too late. I nearly was. You have always told us to train for every possibility. Even the ones you haven't thought of yet."

Adrienne stands regally and garners everyone's attention. Her hair is tied back into a spiraled bun. She changed her clothes from the maid's uniform to that of an elegant movie star. She is markedly attractive, and formidable.

"Dayton is right, Zachariah. Even you must bend to see reason."

Zach is agreeing, and he turns to Esme. "I see I am outvoted on this. And in truth, it is always safer to prepare. I cannot be everywhere at once. And neither can Dayton."

"Good." Esme folds her hands. "And about learning the business? How this thing operates?"

"Dayton can take you around for a tour in the morning, after your training."

"Zach, I've got things to do. I didn't bring your daughter here to continue playing babysitter."

"Said daughter doesn't need you to."

Zach and I ignore Esme.

"As you said before, you are my best operative. Who better than you to teach Esme to defend herself and to show her what we do here at Phantom. Besides, I've got a business to run. And technically, you're still on leave."

Arguing now, in front of Esme, would be futile.

"I'd like to speak with Benson. And Jacque when he gets here. I have some intel on where Molin will be his weakest."

"I'll set it up. Jacque has already sent me an email and will be flying back after a day of rest from the travel. He sounded not at all surprised that you were missing. Sometimes I think he knows you better than I do."

A silence falls over our group—a comfortable silence, mixed with apprehension, excitement . . . and the smell of supper. There is safety in numbers and in some ways, I enjoy those numbers—when I so often dislike them.

"Well, it's been a long day. I think we'll be heading up." Adrienne's voice is as balmy as the night.

"I guess we will. Murder and mayhem can wait another night."

He takes Adrienne's hand as she escorts them out to a hallway. I watch from my place, aware of Esme's stiffening. Before Zach leaves, he says a final good night over his shoulder then on the other side of the doorway kisses Adrienne soundly.

The night cocoons us, though it is suffocating not comforting. Between the island and Madrid, the easy quiet from before was lost. I want to fill the silence, but I don't do small talk. Not for anyone.

Esme murmurs. "Do you think you could walk me back to my room? I think I'll get lost if I go on my own."

Relieved, I gesture toward the doorway Zach and Adrienne used. "It's on my way."

"Great. This place is monstrous."

"Zach doesn't do anything small."

"I've definitely gotten that from him over the last couple years. He's a pretty unique man."

I nod, moving to another hall. Esme follows me at a discreet distance. I wish I didn't want to take her hand so badly.

"He's the best man I know. You're fortunate to have him as your father."

Esme hesitates, I stop and wait for her to respond. When she does, she trails her hand along the patterned wallpaper.

"It would have been nice to grow up with him. I can see him chasing a kid in these halls and spoiling her with too many sweets."

"A nice thought." One I can easily see myself. "We can't change where we come from, but we can change our tomorrows. I read that somewhere."

"Probably on a cereal box."

I laugh—she laughs with me.

"But it's true either way. Zach is a good man and he makes an even better father if you let him. You can trust him."

"You care a lot about him. I like that about you."

Esme's door is just a few away. At the end of the hall in that godawful powder puff room Zach had done up a few years back. If I'm not careful, I'm going to walk Esme up to that door and kiss her goodnight. Only, it won't be one to shut her up or to put her in her place. It will likely consume us. The pang of longing is sharp, and I fight to keep it in check. For our sakes, I need to. But it's becoming difficult for me to deny the feelings I have for this woman who confounds me.

"Tonight was interesting."

Esme stops at her door and sighs, voice light and casual. But her words aren't light at all. Mostly because I sense where she is heading.

"You look tense."

"Tense?"

"Yeah, like a cat with its back up. If you're worried I'm going to try to kiss you, you don't have to worry about it. I haven't thought about it . . . hardly at all."

"Is that so?" I step closer, and stroke her arms. The pull is so strong, I don't know how to stop it.

"Yeah, not at all really." Esme tips her face up, my head angles. My pulse hammers in my ears. I'm going to kiss her and there is nothing I can say, or do. I want this too badly.

As though we've been kissing for years, Esme's arms fold softly around the back of my neck and our mouths meet. Not in the fierce tangle I expect, but worse, because it's tender. We kiss like lovers, storm-tossed souls finally finding rest.

My hands tangle into her hair as the kiss deepens and we press, taking as much as giving, until there isn't enough air—or room between us.

I stop. I rest my forehead against Esme's. The warmth of our kiss is surrounded by the fragrance of lilacs, and I inhale it.

"I suppose that meant nothing." Esme sighs, running her hand down my back.

"Maybe."

"Mmm." Her lips brush my cheek, touch my mouth, and smile against my lips.

"Still nothing?"

Is she trying to challenge me? It's working.

"Keep trying."

My sanity is hanging by a thread. If I was fully aware of what I was doing, I would have stopped. Wouldn't I? I wouldn't have let it get this far. But I can't leave. I don't want to. Kissing Esme is like coming home and I desperately want to do it again and again and again. I need to leave before kissing isn't enough.

"You need to sleep."

"So do you." Esme sighs, finally separating enough I snap out of my drugged stupor. My head is spinning but my feet feel firm on the ground. And it couldn't have come sooner. I need to think this over and quickly—before I either break Esme's heart or dive headfirst into whatever the hell this is becoming.

"Six sharp."

Esme opens her door and stares at me, those blue eyes wide.

"For what?"

"Training. You like me now . . . wait till we hit the gym. I'm told I look best with a pitch fork in my hands. We'll see how you take it."

Esme's soft laugh is sleepy. "I'll see you in the morning."

Yes . . . she will. Even if it kills me.

Chapter 12 *Trump Card*

Esme

Dayton calls me minutes before freaking five in the morning and says something has come up. Plans for an early morning workout are postponed. I mumble an appropriate response before passing back into oblivion. When I get up—a caffeine vampire, I twist my hair into a bun and throw on old jeans with an even older Eagles cut-off tank. The picture of white trailer trash.

Occasionally, my roots show.

Smiling at my crude joke, I go downstairs squinting in the sunlight. I take it personally until I'm in the kitchens. There's a dark chocolate man standing over a stove.

He gives me a once over and without speaking pours me a cup of coffee. As I stare at it, he heads to the fridge and retrieves cream for me. I douse it properly.

"Thank you, kind sir." My voice sounds like it's been sent through a trash compactor.

His smile is bright, and less annoying than the sun—especially with the taste of Arabica beans on my tongue.

"You must be Esme."

"Guilty as charged. Any way I could wrangle a breakfast? I have no idea what time it is. Or even where I am."

"Give some time for the caffeine to work."

"Are you always this kind to scraggly guests?"

He winks. "Only the ones who belong to the boss. How do you like your eggs?"

"Cooked."

"I'll make some toast to go with it. Should take off the last bits of sleep."

"What's your name so I can write you into my will?"

He laughs, warming me as much as the coffee. "Cain Hernandez. I prefer just Hernandez."

"I like it. Very Spanish. I'm assuming you are from Spain then?" What kind of stupid question is that? Apparently, I need more coffee before trying to speak intelligently.

"Si. I love my country. And I love working here. This job pays well and has great benefits. I started as a young man and never left."

I drain the last drop. Before I can speak, Hernandez places a plate of eggs and two slices of sourdough toast in front of me. My stomach growls in full blown starving mode.

"This suits you. Please never leave me." I offer him a flirty smile as I twirl my fork in preparation for decimating the meal in front of me.

"You are a funny one. Like your father."

"Speaking of—" I take a mouthful of eggs, and sigh with pleasure at the taste of fresh basil and tomato. "Where is everybody?"

"Something came up."

"Something business-y?"

"Si. Your father is a busy man. And with Dayton home, there are things that need tending to."

Home. It sounds strange thinking of Dayton's home as anywhere but the island. But I suppose it's true. My mind does a double take at the happiness caused by Dayton's name and I taste it deeply. Thinking about him means thinking about that kiss. And how great it felt. How everything fit with precision. How my bones melted and nothing in the world was as real as his arms banded around me. I should stop thinking until I'm alone, in case I sigh.

"When will they be home?"

"I'm not sure. Mr. Moncleve said it could be supper. Perhaps in the morning."

"Well, that stinks."

Hernandez smiles knowingly. "If you like, you can explore on your own. Enjoy the place without supervision. It might be good to familiarize yourself with your father's prized possession."

"I'm assuming you mean, other than Adrienne."

"His empire comes second to family and always will."

Intriguing. At the very least a way to pass the coming hours of solitude—distracting me from dissecting my every move with Dayton, which I do no matter how badly I try to—let be, let be. I'm no good at casual relationships. But do I know anything about a real relationship and what it's supposed to be like? Carl's face comes to my mind and I wonder if I will ever be able to think of a man and not him.

I think not. I pray I'm wrong.

Hernandez has deserted me and the kitchen is empty. I poke around at my plate. I'm way too full to pick at the leftovers. I drop my napkin on top like a coroner covering a corpse.

I slide off the stool. "Off to see the wizard then."

I explore until there is nothing else to explore. Aside from the rooms which have keypads and locks so high tech they look stupid. But as for the livable portion of the mansion, I have a better understanding of where everything is. And of course, the amount of wealth my father has gained from killing people.

I count twenty bedrooms. Twenty, which does not include those used for the serving staff. There is a ballroom, two casual conference rooms, my father's study, a library, solarium, gym, pool, and lastly, a billiard room. I stop and play a game of one-man pool. I won. To say the mansion is over the top, is to say pigs are pink.

Walking around aimlessly, the house is similar to Dayton's. Except, the floors are marble and it looks designed for an Architectural Digest photo shoot.

I prefer the island. When I run out of things to see, I head back in the direction of my room and close myself off like a star hiding from paparazzi. I am not even guilty about having pilfered chocolate from the kitchens. Today calls for female pampering.

I draw a bath, fill it to the brim with bubbles and soak long enough to cause pruning on my pruning. I paint my nails a shade of coral. It favors Madrid and its warm-hued palette. These relaxing feminine things restore my humanness. My night of being dragged through the gardens, after enjoying roses and wine, is comfortably far away and I'm grateful for whatever took Dayton and my father away to allow me this respite.

When my pampering is complete, I sit on the window seat, in my pajamas, watching the city incrementally slow at the ending of the day. I don't fight the sleep beckoning me. I curl up on the cushioned bench. The smell of Jasmine oil on my skin lulls me to sleep. My last thought is of Dayton. And kissing him.

Dayton

I find Esme sleeping on the window seat, so small, she could easily be mistaken for a child resting after a romp in the yard. Wearing those tiny blue shorts pajamas and

cotton tank plastered in a set of giant red lips, she might as
well be. And she is perhaps, the most devastating like this.

Cautiously, debating over my coming here, I walk
into her room and stop several feet away. Her shoulders
rise and fall with every breath whistling delicately in
tandem with the brush of branches on the windows. A light
wind cools the mansion tonight and makes the air fragrant
with pomegranate—a smell unique to Madrid. Taking a
bolstering breath, I kneel in front of Esme so I can wake
her. But instead of a gentle shake, my hand touches her
cheek and her wild blonde mane. Like touching spun silk.

"Esme." I brush my fingers along her neck, back
into her hair, then let my hand linger on her shoulder when
her eyes open. She studies me—apparently not yet focused.

"Dayton?"

She sits up and I stand, giving us space. My hand
buzzes from touching her skin.

"What time is it?"

"Ten. I just got in with Zach."

She rubs her face. "You canceled on me this
morning. I thought you were going to kick my butt into
shape."

"I was. But had to do a little house cleaning.
Nothing too complicated. But it's all taken care of now so
we can get back to work in the morning. That is if you
aren't too overtired now?"

Esme stands, arching her back. It does
unimaginable things to me. I stare at the ceiling and
think—of the work to be done on the following day—
anything other than Esme and every part of her glistening
in the moonlight.

"Did you have a good day?"

"I did." She pads to a tall lamp and flips it on. Dim
light splashes over the floor and touches the toes of my
shoes. "Aren't you looking dapper."

I glance at my suit. "I do dress for business on

occasion. Today, I needed to play the part."

"How many different parts do you play?"

That's query and challenge. "As many as I need to. Speaking of, I'm still responsible for your welfare and it's obvious you're not getting enough sleep. You look exhausted."

She laughs. "I think we are beyond you as my caretaker. Or do all caretakers kiss their wards?"

I grin. Even here, when anticipation and want are strong, I am able to relax with her. The stress of the day, however small, lessened as I walked into the mansion, and now is long gone

"If I were to kiss you again, it breaks every standard of care imaginable. It could be considered immoral."

"Could it?" She joins me at the edge of the light and I'm struck with how symbolic it is. I stand at the edge of my darkness and she—at her light. For us to be together, in many ways, we must stand with one foot in each world. Her hand finds mine.

"I'm sure of it."

"Then you'd better not kiss me."

"No. I shouldn't." My voice is low.

"Then you'd better not want me," she whispers.

I've already maneuvered her to her toes, one hand pressed on the small of her back to pull her near, the other traces a line on her cheek. "I can't help it."

"That's a good thing, because I can't seem to help wanting you either."

My mouth captures hers. In an embrace of longing, she returns the strength of it, hands gripping the front of my suit, a soft sound of acceptance from her lips. It shouldn't mean so much to want her like this or that she wants the same things. But it does.

"I missed you." My breath rushes out. Esme leans heavily into me, her face nestled against me as if listening to my heart. She won't be able to mistake the hammering of it.

Cradling Esme, I struggle to become nonchalant . . . like the day before I met her and my life was so straightforward, and albeit empty. Can I ever go back? Will it be possible to move on when this is over and know Esme is living, laughing, and perhaps loving, in a different part of the world?

"I missed you too. This place is huge without you." I mumble into her hair. "It's a formidable home."

"Am I imagining this?"

"What?"

"Us. It's . . . different. We've . . . we're—"

"Esme."

She pulls out of my arms. I don't stop her. The desperate neediness in me and fighting for control is far from healthy, it's outright dangerous. I have never needed anyone—and will continue to never need.

I expect a question from Esme I'm not ready to answer, something a logical person deduces as the normal step in a fast growing relationship. That is what we have isn't it? A relationship? I study her profile and know with profound dread what I've known since the wanting of this woman. She is to be my undoing. And this is past the point of a mere relationship. Her eyes swing to mine and I see exactly what I have been afraid of, and could not stop myself from wanting or answering any more than I could stop breathing.

Soul gazing into soul.

"Not tonight." My voice comes out rough like gravel, and Esme nods.

"Should I meet you in the morning then?"

I assess her words like I'm reading through honey.

"No. Not in the morning. I've got work. Make it the day after tomorrow."

Her raised eyebrows warn me of the thin ground I

tread on, and I give her a brief smile, burying the uncertainty.

"Perhaps I should ask my father to get another trainer."

I laugh. "He wouldn't dream of having someone take over the position when his favorite pick is merely delayed by important work."

"Then the day after tomorrow, at the same ungodly hour you wanted this morning?"

I settle into my role as trainer. "Of course. You need all the help you can get."

Esme laughs, and all the tension from before, has vanished. "You have no idea."

I will soon. I hope you sleep well."

"Will you kiss me goodnight?

Must she look so lovely when asking me?

Must she be so tempting to a man trying to do the right thing? My hands cup her face to draw her into a firm press of lips. Our breaths mingle, and we separate as quickly as if she merely bid me a formal goodbye. But her eyes shine with secrets and by the look in them, I have just condemned myself.

"Day after tomorrow. Bright and early."

"Yes."

When the door closes me off from her, there is a physical sigh of frustration—perhaps shared.

Chapter 13 *Pitiless Learning Curve*

Esme

If brutality has a name, it is Dayton Jepsen.

"Faster."

"I'm going as fast . . . as my legs . . . will take me."
I spit out the words between clenched teeth whilst making
my floppy legs eat up ground. If my muscles could fall
from the bones, they would have thirty minutes ago.

Dayton was serious when he said he trains hard. I
made the mistake of underestimating his claim four days
ago. Four torturous, uber-tense days. What was I thinking?
Oh, I want to be like the men and protect myself. I regret
this pro-female power stance now. Most especially as we
close in on my third mile of the morning. I don't run! I do
yoga. Or swim. This—is plain torture!

"As an attacker, I would have caught you minutes
ago. You'd be dead."

Gasping for breath, I stop at the first bend of the
track we've been using and swing around to raise my fists
at him. "You wanna go? Now? Bring it!"

Mistake. The look of victory in Dayton's green eyes
says this is going to hurt.

After a pitiable scramble for control, I give into the
girlish urge to squeal when he hefts me over his shoulder
and tosses me to the grass. My breath is knocked out and I

save my head the majority of the blow. When I hit the ground, my ears are ringing. Likely from exhaustion as well as lack of oxygen.

Dayton lets me roll in a gasping strain, get my air back and then he's sitting on top of my stomach, all six foot-four of him, using only one hand to hold my back flat to the ground. If my position beneath him weren't so humiliating it would be all kinds of distracting. The smell of his aftershave clouds my senses. His mouth is smiling, lips perfectly kissable…body lean and smelling of man with a capital M. Where is my self-control? My focus?

"Damn it. Okay."

"Okay what?" He asks, eyes gleaming, face hardly sweaty.

It's infuriating.

"Okay, get off." I gasp in a breath, try to calm and fail entirely as my voice climbs to a pinched growl. "I'd be dead. I'm totally out of shape compared to you and I suck. I get it."

"You don't suck. But you aren't where you need to be. Getting angry with me for pushing you only leads to this."

"To mortal embarrassment?" I say, bucking beneath him. He is an iron wall, his hand is warm and firm on my collarbone. Distraction . . . thoughts having nothing to do with training.

"In this instance, yes. But overall, I can't help you if you're too angry with me to use what I can give. Anger doesn't help if you don't channel it. So, channel it."

Gifting me with freedom, Dayton rises, offers his hand and I begrudgingly accept it so he can pull me to my feet.

"Are we going to do this every morning? It's been four days. Shouldn't we be doing more by now?"

"Do you want to be able to defend yourself?"

"Yes."

"Then yes. In three weeks, there will be an annual get-together for the Tormina family. I'm sure you know of it—La Grande Caccia."

Every muscle in my body goes on alert at the all-too-familiar name. "The Great Hunt."

"Yes." His eyes travel toward the Phantom headquarters looming beneath the sun. "This is where we can be sure Molin Tormina will be, as well as any of his associates. When the time is right, we plan on a gas leak in the building. Unfortunately, there will be no survivors."

I stare at him, my gut becomes wriggling worms. "And you want me to be ready by then."

"I need you to be ready. I want you to push yourself to the max. They know you're in Madrid and they know we're regrouping. For what, they have their suspicions. And will want to attack first, at any chance. That means being ready."

I'm nodding. "For any outcome. Any possibility."

"You're learning. Good. Because we are heading to the weights. You need to add power to your hits."

Dayton is jogging in the direction of the manor. I fall into step beside him and I am determined not to go into panting. My legs are burning—everything is sort of burning. Even the acid in my stomach is threatening to come up to join the misery party. I never cried from working out too hard, but I'm getting to that point rapidly.

"When do we do the learning to fight?" My voice comes out sounding half-strangled mid-jog, but understandable.

"After the weights, we'll go through some basics."

I try not to be resentful. "Shouldn't I spend most of my time on learning to fight? Not on running and weight lifting?"

Dayton is trying not to laugh, something that makes me wish I had red hair as an excuse for my temper.

"*Fille stupide.* Strengthening your body is strengthening your mind. Doing that, will make you a better opponent and a better fighter, first and foremost. Master the basics, master the art."

He sounds like a poster child for some Kung Fu master.

Reaching the gym, I assume the tripod position to catch my breath, then follow Dayton into the pit of despair, mumbling under my breath. "I'm not a silly girl."

Dayton's response is a deep chuckle that echoes menacingly in the corridor as we descend.

An hour later, post-weights, and 'basics' I am prone on the gym mat wishing to be mercifully put down.

"Kill me now."

Dayton gives me a shove with his foot. "Go shower it off and get some food. I'll meet you in an hour in front of Zach's study."

"Wait." I flop over and dare him to laugh at my tomato red face. "We didn't even kiss yet."

Dayton's eyes are as amused as I hoped they be. During the horror of the hardest workout of my life, I did the best I could not to think about how badly I want to kiss him. All I do is wonder when my fix is going to happen. Sad, but true. We haven't kissed in eighteen hours. I haven't brought up anything about our possible—maybe future plans and thus, we've coasted in a pleasantly frustrating symphony of casual kisses, gentle touches, and avoiding the unavoidable. My affection has done nothing but grow since I met him and I can only pray it's the same for him, because if it isn't . . . I've got me some problems.

When I put my weight onto my elbows, Dayton squats and touches my cheek. "What am I going to do about you, Esme?"

I am warmed by the want I see. There is more than simple desire in his gaze. I feel it, as tangibly as his lips will be on mine.

"Kiss me. You really should kiss me."

He does. It's short, sweet and a tad coarse. Somehow suited to our current states and enough to sizzle me to the core.

"Get cleaned up. I'll meet you in an hour."

"Are we going to talk about this?" I holler to Dayton as he's walking out of the gym.

"I'll think about it."

I'm laughing when I fall back to floor and groan. At least that's something.

Washed, fed, and feeling like a whole new, but somewhat decrepit, woman, I meet Dayton on the dot an hour later in front of my father's study.

The sun is shining, the air is filled with promise and generally speaking it doesn't seem like I'm about to tour my father's mega assassin business. Or whatever one might call this conglomerate of like-minded criminals.

"You clean up nicely."

He smiles. He does not compliment me, though his gaze lingers on my dark navy romper and Keds.

"I have a busy day, so you'll need to keep up."

"I'm ready. What's first?"

"First, I'm going to show you our war room."

"Okay."

I stay close as we maneuver through halls to a pair of doors as thick as my legs. I'm guessing they are soundproof. It is one thing to imagine what my father and Dayton say they do—another entirely to witness it firsthand

"Wow."

"Everything is state of the art and the most secure money can buy." Dayton says.

He leans into an apparent retina scanner. When a light blinks green, the door clicks open.

"I didn't think those things were real." I don't hide my surprise.

"If you can imagine it, it's real. Stay close and out of the way."

I have the ridiculous urge to ask if I can take his hand. What am I, twelve? Instead, I tighten my lips and I try not to fidget when we enter the "War Room."

"Here is the brain of the organization."

And a brain it is. The room is separated into several banks of computers and desks, and each occupied. I count the employees—accomplices? There are ten clicking on keyboards or murmuring into black headsets, the sound produces an odd humming effect. It's like a snapshot out of a spy movie. And I almost laugh out loud.

If Dayton notices how funny I think it is, he doesn't show it, but instead slowly walks the length of the room and explains in a roughened whisper.

"The war room is where orders go for processing, and then are fully detailed, researched, and finally given either approval or rejection. We receive many requests daily and that requires manpower. As does the logistical end of the work. For example, I'm on a job in Buenos Aires and need a hotel as well as a concierge service. These are the people who coordinate it. Without them, we'd be lost."

"Wait, so how many people want to kill other people a day here?"

"I believe we receive upwards of several hundred requests daily. Mind you, those requests are thoroughly vetted. Phantoms do not take contracts that will hurt our reputation or don't have enough cause. After that, it goes to the bull pen for selection."

"Bull pen?"

He nods, pointing to a second set of doors.

"And, what are the parameters for the Phantoms to accept a contract?" A question I should have asked long ago.

He studies me before answering, and I can't help wondering what he's thinking. He must know how curious I am about him and my father and how I'm filling in the pieces as we go. This thing I'm learning about, is a part of two men I'm falling in love with. Thinking it is scary.

"Phantoms never accept a contract to kill a child or pregnant woman."

"A good rule of thumb." I think dry humor is the only way I'm going to get used to this new reality.

"All accepted contracts must have some sort of humanitarian advantage. Meaning, we don't do petty infractions. A husband wanting his wife offed for cheating, an underling wanting his boss ousted for a promotion. We deal in . . . bigger fish only—like government contracts for the worst of the worst."

"You've killed for the government. My government of the U. S. of A?"

He smiles, but his eyes go dull.

"For many governments. As long as there is a good enough reason, it gets sent to circulation. Bids go out to the most prominent operatives first, then if passed up, to the less experienced and so on. Some contracts require teams, others don't. That's part of where the brain comes into effect. We need their help to coordinate resources."

"It's more complicated than I thought."

"Zach didn't get all this way without a good deal of skill and planning. He built it from the ground up. And every rule, every implementation you see, is because of him."

"What sort of reason, is a good enough reason to kill? I want to feel better about this. Help me to."

"Esme, there are many men in this world who shouldn't breathe the same air as the innocents. These men are who we remove. Yes, we get paid for it. And paid well. But what we do, is for the best."

"But you hate it."

"Just because killing doesn't agree me, doesn't mean I don't agree with it. After all these years, I still see the need."

"Judge, jury, and executioner."

We walk toward the double doors.

"To answer your question about the reason to kill, we often take contracts for war lords, crime bosses, drug runners, and sex traffic kings. These sorts of people end up on Interpol or government watch lists. What these organizations can't do to stop them, we can. It's a balanced system in an unbalanced world. Justice for the darkest places a person can go."

I smell the sharp tang of coffee a second before we step into the bull pen. I walk in behind Dayton. The coffee smell gets stronger. I don't need to ask to know he wants to move on. I want to as well. I doubt these things are soaked in at surface level. They need time to percolate and resonate after a great deal of thinking. Perhaps even prayer— if God is willing to listen to an old acquaintance.

"Welcome to the bullpen."

I stare at the bullpen. How is it I am continually surprised that something so uncivilized—is so civilized? This place is for research, work and planning by the chilliest bunch the world has to offer. And it's like a library or some philosophical retreat palace.

The room, decorated in bold rich colors, has one entire wall dedicated to television screens. Each depicts a different news station and there are enough to cover a large part of the globe. I watch the technicolor display and try to focus on what Dayton is saying.

There are no desks with efficient-looking people clicking away at designated positions. There are three tables placed separately like a library offers study places. Each table has a thick swivel chair and a desk lamp, and for convenience, an ashtray and cups filled with pens and sharpies. From our position, there are only two men in the room at the farthest table, facing the windows overlooking the inner courtyard.

Are there any female assassins here? Not that I have any interest in joining the Phantoms. Ever.

Like college students cramming for finals, they hunch over manuals, pens in their hands, and their faces intense. They could be planning for an upcoming contract—and they seem as innocent and friendly as someone you might bump into at the grocery store. Surreal. Outrageous.

"What are you thinking?"

"Thinking?" I say, lowering my voice as if we are in a library.

I think my heart might stop if one of those men looks at me. And what does that say about me? I'm falling in love with the killer at my back but frightened of what he is? Get it straight, Esme.

"It's a lot to take in."

"It can be." His eyes are on mine, searching for something—and I wish I didn't know what that something is. If he is conflicted by the emotions in this tour, then I'm no help.

"So, this is where you came to plan your missions."

"Yes, this is where I came. Where others will come after. It's a quiet room, with good lighting, and excellent internet connections. Good work can be done here."

My mind spins. Good, by definition—*primum non nocere*, Latin. First, do no harm. One of the oaths a medical doctor is asked to take? By that same gradient, is taking a life in order to save others, doing good? According to every history book in the world, the answer is yes. Why else would war, and the ensuing loss of life, be allowed, if not for some higher purpose? My definitions of right and wrong, good and evil are being challenged in their fundamentals. What's worse, it is no challenge at all to say how I'm feeling about the man who is observing me with such awareness.

"What's next?"

He nods at doors that lead to the courtyard. "I can show you the prep rooms."

"What are those about? More research for contracts?"

"No, the research and paperwork are all done in either the war room, bull pen, or the administrative offices. Prep rooms are physical. Hands on busy work. This is where we train. Where you might train, if I can get you up to speed."

"Oh."

"Beyond those, the last thing I can show you is where the records are stored. For each contract, there is a digital copy produced of the work, research, and of course resolution. These copies are kept under lock and key and watched twenty-four seven. The only way we remain at the top, is because we make ourselves unbeatable in efficiency, speed, and of course confidentiality."

I follow Dayton into the warm air and miss the A/C immediately. It's midday now and the heat is balmy but humid.

"You could be a campaign slogan for the Phantoms."

"With a dozen years under my belt, one would hope I could be. I've only got another hour before my meeting with Benson and Jacque, but I think that's enough to finish. Any questions?"

"I've mostly been asking them when they come to me."

"Wouldn't want it any other way."

"No? Don't I talk too much for you?"

"You do. But in the instance of learning, there are no stupid or superfluous questions."

"You'd make an excellent teacher."

I've embarrassed him.

"Something to consider I suppose when the time comes."

I stop inside the doors opposite the courtyard and resist the urge to swipe at my face. Dewy skin is better than red. And with my coloring, it takes little to go red. And if we keep on the path I've sent us, my face may go red quickly.

"When do you think that time might come?"

"Are you asking on a professional standpoint or personal, Esme?"

"Both I guess."

"Professionally, I'm ready to make a change. You picked up on that easily enough, and Zach knows too. Personally . . . I don't know."

For once I see vulnerability.

I step closer, risking rejection when I take his hands. It's like grounding us together might make sense of things. "I like you Dayton. More than I should."

His eyes are so intense on me, a bomb could explode a foot from us and it would be difficult to look away.

"And I like you, Esme. Very much. What are you fishing for here?"

"I—I want to know if you want more from us. If we're headed in the same direction."

"More—"

"More—as in, you'd like more from us? Or more as in a question? Because I can't always read between the lines with you and this whole thing with coming to Spain, seeing the assassin headquarters and facing the death of the entire Tormina family has me scrambling like—"

Dayton presses his finger to my lips. "Shhh. You're making my head spin and I'm not even the one babbling."

"I'm not—"

"Yes, you are. If I take my hand down, will you be quiet?"

My first instinct is to jerk back, and stomp his instep with everything I've got. But I play possum. Being attractive, interesting, and impressive—to the man I may want to spend the rest of my life with—doesn't give him the right to silence me like a naughty child. So, I nod.

"Esme."

Dayton says my name like a prayer.

Apparently, I have a thing or two to learn about how to end an argument before it begins because Dayton rolls over me like I'm water. Brushing the hair back from my face, he rests his forehead on mine and the breath goes straight out of me. I'm frazzled when I smell mint in his breath and sandalwood on his skin. Fresh, masculine and bone melting. I'm helpless as he kisses my nose, my cheeks, my lips, and as though doing his best to savor it all. I curl into him for the sweetness, and passion, and electricity.

I've never experienced this, but with this joy, there is a ripping sensation. Warning, black fear. I'm afraid of losing Dayton. Of this—ending, and with it, the bond that has been forged.

And there is a bond. I taste it in the way he kisses me, I know it in the pressure of his arms as though he has the desperation I do.

When he draws back from me and grins, my heart leaps—then falls.

My God, I'm in love with him. I've only known the man a few weeks, a smattering of days and sure as the sun—I'm in love with him.

"Now, what were you saying?"

He can't know what happened within me. It makes me weak and absurdly exposed, like the whole world could tell. I fight the urge to run from the sun and Dayton.

"I guess you've practiced to perfect that."

"Not as much as you might think. Your thoughts were going so fast you were starting to vibrate. I figured I did you a solid, and slowing them."

"Yeah, thanks. I am so much slower now."

He laughs, tucking my hand into his. We walk to what may be another rabbit trail. If I were alone in this place, I'd become lost, and never find my way out. They'd discover a corpse some weeks later in a remote room on the fourth floor and realize it was me.

"Esme, I like you. You like me. Do we have to know everything right now? Can we keep things simple between us?"

I study him discreetly. The light of the hall reflects on the tile and it makes the floor look wet.

"I don't know how simple things can be under our current circumstances."

"I mean only that I'm just a man. And you, are just a woman. We obviously like each other, are attracted to each other. It could mean everything, or . . . not. What I can tell you, is I've never felt about any woman, what I'm feeling for you. But that means we need to take things slow and to be careful. I don't want to hurt you, but I'm not exactly white picket fence material."

"I'm aware at this point what sort of man you are. But that's not all you're telling me."

"Let's not make this a big deal. Things are good right now and there's a lot going on. We don't need to add anything to our situation."

"Situation?"

"Yes, this relationship between us. We've only known each other for . . . six weeks."

My hands are shaking, so I hide them. "And that makes what's been going on between us any less real?" *Calm yourself. You'll ruin everything.*

"No, but it gets easy for one of us to get caught up. To see things in an unrealistic light. I don't want that for us. Damn it, Esme, I'm trying not to hurt you. Can't you accept that?"

"You think I'll fall head over heels for you and then you'll have to let me down easy." My tears well. Cursed, wretched man.

"That isn't what I said."

"I heard what you said. If you can't handle a commitment then you shouldn't have started anything with me, Dayton."

"It's not about a commitment. I'm perfectly capable of remaining loyal to one woman. That isn't what this is about, why are you twisting things around?"

"I'm not twisting things. I'm merely reading between the lines. And what I read is, you want something fun and easy. No strings." I tense as he takes a step closer. "But I'm not that kind of woman. If I gave you the wrong impression about me, then I'm sorry. But I don't do things half-assed."

"Esme, this is ridiculous! One minute you want things between us to be good and then, you don't want it unless it's your way? That isn't the way life works. Things are messy. I'm messy. I don't know what to say to you."

"There isn't anything to say. We've said plenty. I think I need some air."

"Wait."

"No! Let me be, Dayton. I need to be alone."

"You don't know the way back."

"I'll manage." I walk faster. Tears are dripping by the time I get to the hall.

Chapter 14 *Waiting Game*

Dayton

I've given Esme three days. And it has cost me every night, every day and everything in between.

I was distracted during my meeting with Jacque and Benson—an unforgivable blunder. Little progress was made though the plans were outlined and the blueprints obtained. Getting the explosives into place will be tricky, but not impossible, particularly with an inside contact— which I'm working on and will likely have by the end of the day.

These things take time and patience. An attention to detail and single-minded focus. But I can't focus. I can't do anything but think of Esme, and then feel like a fool for doing so.

She is the one being ridiculous. She is the one who basically demanded a swearing of fealty on bended knee and bright future in hand. I can't give her those things, I don't even know if I can guarantee her the next month. But each time I close my eyes, I see hers and it cuts me.

She frightens me.

Admitting such, even to myself is a disgrace all its own. Particularly to a man who swore to never put himself in this position—and yet, here I am. Exactly between the rock and hard place I didn't want to be.

I never thought I'd meet a woman worth spending the rest of my life with, and I certainly didn't expect to meet one with the whole package—I didn't even know I wanted a package. My God, a few weeks ago, I was certain I would die a single, old, and happily alone crone on a Caribbean island in the Dominican Republic. And now, well now, for bloody sake, I'm contemplating how I can grovel to get my boss's daughter to speak to me. If it weren't so pathetic, it would be humorous.

Because I want her to be the one. Because everything she is hinting is exactly what I envision. But that's like a mirage, an impossible image. I've never had family, except for Zach. I've never truly loved anyone. Not really. For a very long time, the idea of love seemed a myth. I am relieved to know I can love at all. I found Zach and he showed me what a family could be and how love can be shown or given.

But to love a mate, the sort of love that supposedly transcends everything including time and circumstance . . . I don't know if it's a real thing. Can I say I'll stay with Esme no matter what? Yes, but that isn't what she's looking for. She wants a soul promise. The kind a husband gives to a wife he actually loves with everything in him. More than himself. The love verified by a priest before God. And I dread to know what God thinks of me, Zach's words on the subject aside.

I don't know if I'm capable. Or if all the years of violence, brokenness and emotional wasteland have ruined me for the sort of love Esme is searching for. And this, above anything else, has made me angry . . . with myself for letting this happen, and with Esme for making me want to—for making me question my sanity and wanting to beg to see her.

Pitiful. Shameful.

I'm going to beg.

Cursing under my breath, I stalk the length of the fourth floor and stand in front of Esme's door. I contemplate leaving, then give three short knocks. She doesn't answer.

"Esme, I need to talk to you. At least give me a chance to do that."

"Dayton? Are you looking for Esme?"

I whirl, caught, and I try to appear casual. Zach looks amused as he withdraws a cigar from his breast pocket. Of course, Zachariah must know of the way things have progressed between his daughter and me, likely even our fight, but I'm like an ant under a microscope as he watches me with a self-satisfied grin. "She's out with Adrienne. They went shopping."

"Oh. It's nice they're getting along."

"Yes, it is. Adrienne told me Esme is as sweet as her letters. I'm tempted to pinch myself. It's a dream."

I'm aware of Adrienne's inability to have children, I didn't realize how much that mattered to Zach and how glad he is to have a child, though full grown, of his name.

"She is lovely."

"*Oui. Belle et charmante.*"

I wonder at what point Zach is going to let me escape with a modicum of my manhood intact. Currently it's hanging by a thread.

"Come share a drink with me. We can talk about what you did to anger Esme."

I'm very tempted to escape through the window. There is only so long I can avoid talking to Zach about this. He's going to find out, although he probably already knows more than I want him to.

"In this case, it's mutual."

"I suspected so. It always takes *deux.*"

"I'm learning very quickly what it takes. The hard

way."

"It is the way of men. We learn nothing easily when it comes to women. Come, we will commiserate over a bottle of Chianti."

We take over the library and settle into the twin wing-back chairs like groaning senile men. Chianti is not my first choice of wine, but I've never wanted liquid courage more. Speaking from the heart in depth is Zach's spiel, not mine. I don't enjoy it.

"Benson tells me Esme is excelling in her training."

"Benson?"

That infuriating woman! How could she go behind my back and use another trainer? Yet, after our argument and obvious entanglement, how could she not? I'm not above swallowing humble pills, but it's difficult to do now.

"Yes." Zach puffs on his cigar. "She asked me to place him with her after your spat. I obliged and said nothing, as any father might give his daughter some privacy."

"But you've decided to break that silence now."

"Of course. I've waited long enough and she is my daughter, after all."

I catch the undercurrent of conflicting emotions.

"We see things differently. It creates problems."

"This isn't a test Dayton. Don't answer me in that ambiguous tone you use for a diplomat. What exactly went wrong? And while we are on the subject, what are you going to do to fix it?"

"She wants a commitment from me. Or at least, a statement of my intentions. I apparently, am like all the other males—and am not ready to give absolutes yet. We haven't been seeing each other long enough. My feelings are complicated—as are our futures."

"Mmm, and what makes them complicated? Do you enjoy her?"

"Well, yes, but—"

"Find her attractive?"

"Yes, Zach, but you're missing the point."

"Am I?" Zach leans forward in his chair. "I am sensing a great deal of fear in you. Fear breeds poor decisions based on unrealistic perceived obstacles."

I am awkward discussing hurdles in my relationship with Esme, considering the man across from me is her father. Unreal doesn't even cover it. I'm well aware Zach doesn't miss the bitter tinge in my voice.

"What are you, Yoda?"

"Sarcasm won't hide you any better, Dayton. It is uncomfortable pinning you down like this, *oui*? But it is necessary. I would be speaking to you in this way if it was not my daughter on the receiving end. But seeing that is how it is? Well, it makes my stake in it more valuable. I care, deeply about the outcome. For you both."

I gulp the Chianti. It doesn't help the desert in my mouth.

"I think . . . I think I might be falling in love with her. But the problem is, I don't know. And that's not enough for Esme."

"Have you told her this? That you think you are falling in love?"

"Not in those words. I told her I cared about her. And I didn't want to overcomplicate things—"

"Then how do you know if it is enough? What did you say to make her run so quickly?"

I think over what I said for the umpteenth time and wince now that I hear it clearer.

"I said I wanted to keep things simple between us. Because I'm not sure how things might progress."

"I suspect she did not take this well."

"No. Esme said I am trying to avoid committing so I could just have fun. Which is as far from the truth it could get. But how can I explain something I don't understand? I don't know if I'm capable of giving her what she needs."

I stand, leaving the wine, and stare into the fading sunlight. The pain in my head is enough to cloud my vision, and I wonder if speaking with Zach is a mistake.

"How do you know what she needs Dayton?"

"I just know, all right? She's a good woman. With morals and a clear code. She made an honest success for herself and aside from this business with Carl, she's snow white. She doesn't belong with a man like me. She wants a house, with the picket fence and a few babies. Who wouldn't? But I'm none of those things. I'm a sinkhole. I barely have a handle on my life and though I've made excellent money, could I ever actually father children for her? Raise them in a place where they will always be safe from what I've done for over a decade? I come from nothing. And I have nothing to offer."

When the silence falls between us, it's heavy but warm.

"That you are thinking about these things, is sign enough of how you feel. You only have to admit it to yourself."

"Damn it, Zach, stop speaking like a psychiatrist for once and be a man. What the hell do I do about it?"

Zach's voice is soft. "You do whatever is necessary. First, reconcile your heart with what it already knows. And second, brush up on your groveling. Flowers usually help ease the birthing pains."

"I . . . I need to think."

"There is nothing to think about. If Esme were to leave tomorrow to never come back, would you tell her then? Would you let her see what you are so afraid of showing?"

I close my eyes, and I'm struck with the absurdity of what I know I will do. What I would have done had it not been put so simply.

"Yes. I would tell her."

"Good boy." Zach is at my side and his hand

squeezes my shoulder reassuringly. "I'll give you a few pointers about how to make up properly to the woman of your dreams."

I'm going to need them.

Esme

"Can we talk of Dayton now? Or am I to continue pretending he doesn't exist?"

Adrienne has been nursing a diet coke for the last hour as we talk about everything except Dayton, and the sigh falls from me like a bandage on a wound.

"You've been moping around the house for three days."

"I haven't been moping. Well, maybe some. But I've been dealing with a lot lately." I study my five shopping bags stashed in the empty chairs.

"Code for, dealing with Dayton?"

"Well, yes. He is a lot. But that hasn't been the only thing on my mind. The Ball is growing closer and with it, my anxiety is climbing."

Adrienne plucks a croissant from a tray with manicured fingers. She wears all white, with a large brimmed Marilynn Monroe type hat and chic oversized sunglasses. "Dayton is so like Zach at his age. In many ways, they are mirror images of each other."

"Dayton? I don't see it."

"He has soft places too . . . like anyone else. I think he covers them better than most. Zachariah prefers to wear his heart on his sleeve, an amiable quality and leaves his temper for the rest. And mind you, that temper is strong when provoked.

Dayton is the same. Though his heart is hidden, and he becomes provoked less often, he is equally passionate and loving. The men seek adventure in their very bones, and will likely die some day for it."

I sip my soda. The idea of Dayton ever dying makes me want to weep.

"Well, it doesn't matter now. We've broken things off. We aren't on the same page or wanting the same things. A non-starter."

"I don't believe that."

"You should. Dayton told me he wanted to keep things simple and unattached. Code for, I'm just not that into you and don't want to commit."

"Dayton has no problem with committing. That isn't the issue. He's hiding."

"Hiding? He'd never be caught dead hiding from anything."

"Oh. Well, that's interesting. You love him."

Hearing something so private spoken out loud, my face grows warm.

"I guess. Yes." Saying it out loud changes nothing. "Yes, I suppose I do."

"Then you should fight for him. Especially when he has no idea what's good for him."

"I'm better at the old-fashioned way of letting the man take the reins."

Adrienne laughs and the sound is robust and feminine. It makes me smile and relax further into my seat. The last week and a half have proven her a female companion and ally. In a world dominated by violence and confusion with primarily men, our blossoming friendship is invaluable.

"Of course, you are a woman, it is natural. I'm not suggesting you battle Dayton to the ground and force his hand, but rather . . . use your feminine wiles to illuminate a failing on his part. To make it obvious what he is missing."

"And that is?"

"That he is madly in love with you, darling. What else? Give him some time, increase the pressure and when he is ready, make him grovel. It will do him good to realize how he needs you."

I laugh. "I uh, need to ask you a favor then . . . how do I increase the heat or pressure, I have no clue how to do it and to be blunt, I've never had to."

Adrienne's smile is feline as she cocks her head and tips her sunglasses on her nose. It's unsettling and hope-filling at the same time.

I've been nothing but miserable going over what I said to Dayton, how I might have reacted, if I should be the first to end our stalemate. I didn't know what to do. And I about resigned myself to a life of pining and crying jags before this little war strategy. Now, I'm trying to subdue the surge of hope, but it's contagious as Adrienne leans in and lays out a plan to remind Dayton of what he wants.

I pray to God he takes the hints, because if he doesn't, then I'm going to move to the Italian countryside when this is done, buy ten cats, and live out my days as the spinster no woman ever wants to become. Because I can't see living without Dayton. He's the one. Now, he needs to see that.

Chapter 15 *Wolf in the Hen House*

Mr. White

I've waited the full length of the day for Esme to return and even longer for an opportunity to leave early from my duties. Although gaining access into the Moncleve empire was difficult, it has proven fairly easy to roam about the villa and outbuildings with little censure.

I can snap a man's neck with one hand in about four seconds, but I've been granted a position in the janitorial team to clean bathrooms and locker rooms. It's laughable—but necessary. All things must be done for the cause. And this cause is certainly one worth fulfilling.

The sunlight is dwindling by the Jarama riverside. I scan the opposing shore for a white yacht named the Zonnebloem, Sunflower. Molin likes his flowers. Though originally, I am not from the Netherlands, I speak Dutch, French, English, and Spanish rather fluently. My home, Vancouver, Canada, seems a million miles from this culture—saturated part of the world. But I don't miss it.

Studying the other boats docked in the slips, I walk casually, making eye contact with few, but taking in every detail. It's my job. I'm good at what I do. And when the Tormina family asks me for a job, I fly out and take care of it. For a price. Always a price.

Today, my price comes in the form of a fat deposit

in my offshore accounts and a guarantee that I get another installment when the package is delivered. And of course, I intend to deliver. It's what I do. Because I'm the best in the business at retrieval and delivery.

"Took you long enough."

I don't care which member of the Tormina family comes to speak with me, as long as I get paid. *"Heerlijk om te zien dat je bent nog steeds uit en over, na het ongeval en alle."*

"De dwaas! English only! We don't want to take any chances. You're costing us enough, you should know better."

"Excuse me. I didn't realize there were eyes and ears everywhere."

The man gives me an angry look and I ignore it, sighing as I withdraw several photos from my pocket. "She's there. As we predicted and of course well-kept. She sleeps in the most fortified room in the joint under constant watch with security roaming the hall at all hours. It will be tricky to pull her. Especially when she and Dayton Jepsen are such an obvious item."

"I don't want to pull her. I want you to take Jepsen."

I shove the photos back into my pocket. "Dayton is a well-trained operative. His capture will be at least double the price."

"I don't care what it costs. I want him."

"Out of professional curiosity, how bad does your face hurt?"

I dodge a swift jab at my throat and swing out of danger. I laugh straightening my jacket. "Touchy I see. Forgive me. I understand what happened was tragic. I'd be pretty bloodthirsty myself. Now, about the fees, will Molin agree to double them?"

"He'll agree to whatever I want. And I want Dayton."

"Professional curiosity—what do you plan to do when you get him?"

The man laughs, his voice roughened by years he doesn't wear. "When I take Dayton, make no mistake, my little piggy will come squealing and when she does, it will be all the way home."

I nearly shiver at whatever outcome I'm going to deliver to Dayton and Esme. However, that feeling is temporary and like I said—nearly shiver. Money soothes all woes, of this I am a testament.

"I can do it as soon as you'd like."

"I'll be in contact. The money will be wired twenty-four hours before the job needs to be done. And it will get done, is that clear?"

"Of course."

"Don't make any mistakes."

Esme

Armed with phase one of my plan, I am better than the day before and even somewhat cheerful. The sun in Madrid is brighter than usual today. The birds seem happy to be swooping around, twittering and playing with one another. And who could blame them? The world is full of possibilities.

I remember the gray ones are called partridges. And the others, the fat ones with speckles, are hazel grouse. I'm far from an ornithologist, but I think I'm picking up the habit of birdwatching from my father. I guess we do share some interests. It makes me smile on my way through the courtyard, cutting through the grass to reach the gym.

My smile fades as quickly as it takes me to see the man dipped in stretches by the bench press is not Benson. I'm very tempted to feign illness and go back to my room, I have to remind myself of the plan. And of course, as Adrienne so aptly put, of my womanly strengths. Thinking of this, I saunter toward Dayton and add a gentle toss to my hair when I stop in front of him.

"Good morning Dayton, nice day for sweating, don't you think?"

It's ridiculous to pretend our last words didn't end with me running off in tears, but—I'm going to pull off the show of a lifetime.

He looks up at me and my heart does a skip. He doesn't appear to see through the veneer. Step one, appear unaffected and happy. A woman does not need a man to be happy. This will confuse and otherwise anger said male target.

"Good morning, Esme. It's been a long few days."

"It's been a breeze for me. I've been busy actually. Benson even gave me a sterling report yesterday. Apparently, I've mastered my defensive tactics. Makes me gung-ho to learn those offensive ones."

Dayton's gaze narrows and I head for the treadmills. I don't want to lay it on too thick.

"We'll do three miles today, medium pace, forty percent incline."

"Benson had me doing four miles. It wasn't so bad." A muscle twitches beneath his eye.

"Okay, let's do four. Pace yourself so you don't get winded. When you're done, we'll do calisthenics then work on some offensive tactics. Since you've mastered the defensive so well."

There's a glint in his eyes and I regret my rash decision to take on four miles to prove myself when my lungs start burning at mile two. By the time mile four comes around into focus, I'm sweating so badly it's dripping everywhere and my breath is sobbing out of my lungs in horrible dry rasps. Slamming the power button, I just about collapse from the treadmill, but save face by propping myself on the wall for support.

"See?" I slurp in a breath. "Easy peasy. I've been

doing wonderfully with Benson. He's a great teacher."

Give compliments, even unnecessary ones to other young and attractive men. This will create jealousy and/or anger in the male target. He will have the urge to either correct your behavior or prove himself. Both will result in getting attention and increasing want for emotional or physical intimacy. If Adrienne could write a book on torturing the male sex, she'd sell a million in a breeze.

If I'm not mistaken, this is an angry male target. Jaw flexing, eyes narrowed on me, Dayton stops writing on the white board across the room and rolls his neck. His bullet points on conversion therapy are apparently not as important as his question.

"What else did Benson tell you?"

"Oh all sorts of things. He's very knowledgeable." I bend over, touch my toes and try not to squeal in pain. I'm so tight, there should be a new word for what I feel. In truth, I liked Benson, but he'd been too dry in humor and a little lacking in his drive to push me. He treated me with kid gloves and I didn't care for it.

"I'm sure he is. Perhaps you should have been working instead of having all of these conversations."

"Oh we did work too. He's great at multi-tasking." I pull one ankle to my butt for a deep quad stretch. I'm incredibly pleased my smile is firmly in place while doing so.

Dayton doesn't say anything else until we finish calisthenics, consisting of me landing on my face several times after instructed to do a handspring. I might be fit but my range of gymnastics ends at the point of ridiculous. Even so, I work harder than ever and let Dayton's anger guide us deeper into the 'zone'. It's a fiery place, filled with pain and chants of mercy, but I join him gladly because I can see how well Adrienne's plan is working. I think if I say Benson's name one more time, Dayton might wring my neck like a wet gym towel.

Finishing a set of reps with a pair of eight-pound dumbbells, I wait until Dayton is stretching on the large black mats before sidling up to him to do the same.

I'm aware my tactics are petty. And worse, the sort of the thing one might think a vicious scorned woman might do. I don't care. Not when Dayton's eyes rush up to meet mine with pure shock as I stretch into a split with ease. I never said I'm not flexible.

Grinning at him, stifling a laugh, I adjust my ponytail and prop my hands on my hips. "What's next? Combat? You said we could do some offense."

"Uh . . . yeah."

"So, are you going to teach me some hand to hand or . . .?

Dayton looks away from my legs and scowls. "Esme, I think you've done enough for today. I've worked you hard."

"True." I stick my legs out in front of me and fold so I can grab the arches of my feet. I am a red sweaty mess. But I'm hoping beyond hope I am managing to pull off 'glowing' rather than merely leaking all over the mats. "I don't know about you, but I could so use a shoulder massage. Hell, any massage. I've got my hurt on. Big time. Between you and Benson, I feel used up."

I sit up so I can beam my brightest at him. He's already standing, guzzling half a water bottle.

"You wouldn't mind rubbing them, would you?"

He chokes on the water, then wipes his mouth. "What?"

"My shoulders. They hurt pretty bad with all the arm work we've been doing and I could use a little rub. Like ten minutes. I'd be willing to pay someone at this point."

"I don't think that's a good idea."

"Why not? We're good, aren't we?"

"About that, we need to talk."

"We did talk, and it was clear." It's a real effort to keep my tone light and carefree. "I'm only asking for a rub. If you aren't interested, Benson said he'd give me a good rubdown any time I asked."

"That man isn't touching one inch of you."

I raise my eyebrows, though internally the joy buzzes around like bees. "Why not?"

"Because there is a lot we didn't talk about between us and you know things aren't totally resolved."

"We never said anything about not seeing other people. Actually, we never laid out any formal anything between us. Because we never were an item. We were a kind of flirtation."

His eyes are stone. Molten stone. "That wasn't what you hinted at three days ago."

"I must have gotten my head on straight. Benson helped with that."

"Stop saying his name."

I cock my head, wetting my lips. "So, what exactly do you think we are then? I was under the impression it was no big deal. We called it quits."

Dayton's face is red—from anger. He's on the edge. All I need to do is nudge him. But I need to be careful of how and when I do it.

"Don't play the fool. You know we're still something. I've done nothing but think about what we are for the last three days, so don't go changing your story."

"Dayton, I don't want to fight. I want a shoulder rub. I didn't think it would cause such a problem. I'm sorry." The threat of me going to Benson for a massage is thick in the air.

I stand, reach for my water bottle and towel and head toward the doors.

"Wait just a damn minute."

"What for? I don't want to fight, you clearly do."

"Just stop moving." One calloused hand stops my exit and twirls me around to face him. I'm now staring at a broad chest. I lift my gaze and feel all the things I did three days ago and I'm suddenly weak. I would give anything to curl into Dayton. To let him cradle me with those ridiculously large arms and listen to the sound of his heart.

But I don't do those things. No, for the purpose of winning his heart, I lift my chin and don my haughtiest expression. I pray he doesn't see the wash of traitorous tears burning my gaze.

"What now, Dayton? I just want a damn shoulder rub. And I'm going to get it. With or without you."

"Fine."

Anger makes his mouth hard and his hands become rigid. He turns me around. I suck in a breath and don't let it go until he is kneading the desperately achy muscles of my back. I really did need a massage!

I lean into the rub, biting my lip trying not to groan when he digs his thumbs in my shoulder blades and encourages the muscles to relax. He would make a fine masseuse any day of the week.

"This is amazing." I sound drugged. And I drop my water and towel on the floor.

"Great." He snaps.

I close my eyes as he works my neck into submission, then angrily my shoulders. A man can't be this angry at a woman unless he loves her, right? Please God, let that be true.

Dayton pats my back like he would a good horse, I sigh, rolling my shoulders with ease. "Wow. You could make a career out of this."

"Glad to hear it."

He sounds livid. *Temper is the easiest way to break a man*. Then I'm on track.

With a languid smile, I gather my things and stop short of the door. Dayton has made no attempt to follow me. Rather, he remains like a statue, his eyes boring holes into me, hands resting in the pockets of his running pants.

"Will you have dinner with me tomorrow?"

"Have dinner with . . . you?"

"Yes." I laugh. "That's what I said. I'd like to make sure we're all right."

"What do you mean?"

"Oh you know, make sure we can be friends. I wouldn't want things to be awkward between us now. It would be my way of saying thank you for everything and giving us a fresh beginning. As friends."

Anger is now bewilderment. And I should regret the way I'm playing with him, but, I can't. Not now. I'm in the thick of the game and the name of the game is—win. Adrienne assures me this is the route to go.

"Friends."

"Yes, you are repeating me like you don't understand what I'm saying. Are you okay Dayton? You're pale."

"You want to have dinner to be friends."

"Yes, Can you come? I'd like to have it on the roof. Zach tells me the view is magnificent at night. Say seven? I'm going to ask the cook to make something native to Spain. I know how you like cultural diversity in your meals."

It's clear he wants to say no. Or to question what has changed. What has made me so ready to throw everything away between us? As if I could.

"Sure."

"Great. Seven then. Don't be late. See you!" I try to sound cool, and not just relieved.

When I get to the courtyard, I want to collapse from exhaustion—as if I've run a mental and physical marathon. I suppose I have.

Dayton

The woman is playing mind games with me. And I'm the bleeding pawn to her queen.

First, at the gym this morning, mentioning Benson every other sentence, then stretching and flaunting in front me. And the most confusing frustrating conversation about a relationship she is pretending no longer means a thing but was a thing . . . I'm sounding like a woman in my mind. I mull over the last tidy box she gift-wrapped for me. The lady decided to blindside me with dinner. And not just any dinner, no, a dinner to be 'friends'. What the hell kind of man does she think I am? Does she think I could ever just be friends with her after what we've shared?

Anger roils in my stomach as I hit the heavy bag. It sways at the impact. "Stakker!"

Once I'd been able to think past the haze of red this morning, I sought Esme. She was unavailable. What the woman needs with another shopping trip is beyond me. But if her desire to toy with me is to make me angry? Mission accomplished. I'm angry.

I smash my fist into the bag and deliver two short jabs. Fire bursts in my knuckles. I ignore it. I've gone this long before and survived. I'll do it again.

She thinks she can pretend friendship? She's going to learn the hard way what it is to come head to head with a Jepsen. We don't give up easily and we certainly don't scare off when a tiny blonde wants us too . . . or pretends she wants us too.

I drop the boxing mitts on the floor followed by an aggravated growl. I'll go to her little dinner. I'll play along. But I have no intention of walking away as friends with the woman I've finally decided I'm in love with.

Chapter 16 *Ghosts and Demons*

Esme

The waves are warm on my skin. The moon, a hazy orb that dances near the line where sea meets sky and I float aimlessly beneath it. The water is like a blanket around me—comforting and I close my eyes reveling in the smell of summer.

Summer on the island. Dayton's island.

Smiling, I stroke lazily through the water, kicking my feet, letting water trail through my fingers like gossamer film. In this wedge of peace, there is nothing here but me and the water. Nothing but softness and a calm only achieved by water and waves.

I float like this for what seems like hours, but maybe it's minutes or seconds? I can't tell. Time doesn't exist here. Nor does any danger or fear. Just the water and me. Me and the water.

And Dayton.

I can sense him joining me before I sense the movement by my face and I slowly stand on the sandy bottom. It's like satin between my toes and makes me feel like a little girl playing in a ribbon box. I always imagined my Nana would have ribbons and lace beside a sewing machine. But I don't have a Nana. Or a mother. Or a father.

Dayton takes my hand in his and smooths his thumb over the back of it, he smiles gently, his green eyes luminous and bright. "Why are you out here?"

"It's safe out here. Warm and safe."

He watches me a moment, then dips to press a kiss to my mouth, laced with comfort. I take his comfort and give some back, wrapping my arms around his neck, reaching onto my toes so I can feel the full contours of his body.

When he draws back, it is only a breath away, enough to see eye to eye.

"Are you sure?"

My eyes are heavy . . . and drugged "Of what?"

"Are you sure it's safe out here?"

"Of course it is. You're here, aren't you?"

Dayton's body quivers, skin crackles like a molting snake. And I startle back from him, landing hard on my feet, the sand is hard as stone. "What's wrong Dayton?"

"Esme . . . Esme . . . ."

Dayton's face wriggles and grows like a mask— Carl. And I open my mouth to scream. But nothing comes out. Nothing comes out all, because Carl is suddenly on top of me and we are beneath feet of water. There is no air down here. But I can hear him laughing at me, his fingers are tight as a vice on my throat. I'm going to die. I'm going to die under here with Carl.

I lurch awake on the bed sputtering for air, hands clawing at my throat. Panicked, I suck in several breaths, forcing my eyes to see and my mind to understand I'm not underwater—but I'm struggling.

It felt so real. It does every time I dream of Carl, but this was different. Because Dayton had been there and I was on his island. My throat closes with emotion and I clutch the bedspread beneath me, determined not to cry. And I'd been happy. We were really happy.

I won't be able to sleep. Not after such a terrible dream. So I slip into the thick terry cloth robe I use after a bath, tucking my feet into the marshmallow like slippers I so love and shuffle out to the quiet hallway.

It's dark—as if a black sheet is draped over the world. No nightlight to mark the way and no light through the window. It's a new moon tonight. For some reason, I'm grateful for it. The less like my dream it can be—the better.

Feeling my way, I grip the railing like a woman prepared to battle demons, and I feel in many respects I am. Carl's little surprise visit in my dreams has me rattled. I'm raw and reminiscent of a woman I don't want to remember.

I let loose a shrill scream when a shadow emerges at the bottom of the stairs, distinctly human.

"*Esme, sacre merde*! It's me, you're father."

I catch my breath. "I'm sorry."

Zachariah watches me with worried eyes and then sighs like an old man after a trying day.

"I don't suppose you'd like to join me for tea in the study."

"It's three in the morning."

His smile is quick and infectious. Just a while ago, I was terrified out of my mind, sitting in tangled sheets and slicked with sweat. Now, I'm smiling at the man I'm becoming accustomed to calling my father. He has a gift of putting others at ease with little effort—in this case, suggesting tea. Did I truly come from such a man?

"I won't tell, if you don't."

He offers me his elbow. A picture-perfect moment for the estranged father and daughter. "It's no wonder Adrienne fell for you. You're all charm when you want to be." I take his arm.

"A true Frenchman always is."

We walk in silence to his study. I sink into one of the wingback chairs and tuck my legs under me. Zach walks about the room quietly, turning on the fireplace with a switch, then meandering to the shadows by his desk. He's rummaging through cabinets. A hissing is followed by a strange popping sound that draws the most curious of conclusions.

"I hope you aren't a purist."

Zach already has a steaming cup of tea in front of me. I take it with a wistful sigh, inhaling the smell of spicy cinnamon and chamomile, a gentle blend for sleeping. I'm not a big tea person, but I can definitely understand the desire to be. Tea can be used for more than the palate.

I watch Zach settle into his own chair . . . and he solves the mystery of the strange hissing and crackling.

"I used the hot water off the Keurig."

"I'm not very particular when it comes to tea."

"Me either. You like coffee then?"

"With hordes of milk and sugar. If that's even considered coffee then."

He grins over his mug. "A woman after my own heart." He takes a delicate sip, sighs, and relaxes deep into the cushions.

"*S'il vous plait*, tell me what is troubling you. Is it Dayton?"

"No. Dayton and I are working on things, and we are at an impasse. But I'm hoping by tomorrow night we'll be on the same page."

"Oh?"

"I'm sure you've already heard everything from Adrienne."

"It's different from my only daughter. Besides, I'm a romantic. Do you love him?"

My stomach bottoms out, then the warmth of knowing I love Dayton—more than I thought could ever be- -floods through me. "You're the second person to ask me, and it doesn't feel normal to say it out loud. Like I'm going to jinx something."

"There is no such thing."

"So you believe in fate?"

"*Oui,* of course. I believe some are destined for love, others no. But every action, every decision we make, is for a purpose and reason. A greater design."

"By some God?"

"By the one and only God. But yes, that is a discussion for another night and another drink."

Knowing there will be another night to share tea and spill my guts over a burning hearth with my father makes me irrationally . . . gooey. This revelation fills my heart full to the max. I resist standing to hug him like I might have as a child.

"Yes. I love him. Truly love him."

"Then he is a fool not to marry you at once."

I laugh, nearly sloshing my tea on to my lap. But it is so good to laugh! It makes my nightmares crawl further from my mind, and the warmth of the fire and my father's presence stronger.

"It is good to hear you laugh."

"It's good to do it." I hesitate, bracing as I tell him. "You're good for me Zach."

Zach sets his mug on an ebony end table.

"Esme, you've never asked about your mother and me."

I stiffen. It's a topic I don't think I'll ever be prepared to hear. "Is there a need? I know who my mother is. And what she did."

"*Oui,* she made bad decisions, but at a time when we were young and foolish, she was a different woman. She was *belle* and I was a rake."

I mirror Zach's expression. "She isn't a part of the woman I am today. I've met her a handful of times but she didn't raise me. The foster system did."

A storm of regret floods Zach's gaze. "*Je suis désolé.* I would change it if I could."

"I know. You didn't even know I existed until two years ago. None of it was your fault."

His eyes darken and the same ferocity that lives in Dayton surfaces in my father. Adrienne said they were very similar in nature. In this moment, I believe it.

"I was a foolish boy. I slept with your mother knowing full well what could happen and then ran away back to France. A great deal of your upbringing is my fault."

"I don't hold you responsible."

"Why not?"

The sorrow in Zach's gaze stops my breath, and I reach for his hands.

"The past, is in the past. I don't live there and neither do you. We might do things differently had we been able to, but we can't now. I'm willing to move on and let be, let be."

Zach's eyes are watery amber.

"Besides, I have you now, Papa, *oui*? It is all that matters."

This is not the first time I have called Zach father, but to call him something meaningful, truly heartfelt, is a first for us. It suits him better than I ever dreamed. Dare I hope that I have finally found the allusive unit we call family, or believe this ache is as potent as the love I have for Dayton?

His reaction is how any little girl might hope a lost father's to be. Without words, Zachariah Moncleve, gathers me up to embrace me. His arms as strong as Dayton's, are like steel around my waist and the smell of chamomile, cinnamon, and cedar clings to his skin. Tears burn my eyes. I hug him as some part of myself finally, blessedly, molds into place.

As if, I've been waiting for this particular moment for the last twenty-five years.

"Precious Esme." Zach's hands frame my face and he kisses both my cheeks, eyes swimming and mouth smiling wide. "I have you now too. And I love you. *Je t'aime tellement.*"

I struggle but reciprocate the kissing my father's cheeks. I feel a little silly when I do it. What the hell . . . I'm going all out tonight.

"I love you too."

I sit back on my heels, realizing I ended up on the floor in order to hug Zach. Strangely, either it is too late to care or I'm riding on a fluffy cloud of post-reunion bliss, because I settle onto my butt and laugh at myself.

"You should get some sleep."

"*Oui*, but I don't want to yet. Do you mind if I enjoy the fire a while longer.

He bends to kiss my hair. "No. Stay as long as you like. There are a few good books hiding somewhere in those shelves."

I wait until my father reaches the doors, the tails of his robe brushing the marble, his face pink and eyes bright with mischief. I really do love him.

"Papa?"

He stops, with his hand on the brass knob. "*Oui?*"

"Nothing. I just wanted to say it again. It feels good."

Zach grins, leaning on the door, looking like a man lifted of a heavy burden. It's amazing to know I did that.

"It does. Goodnight, *mon chéri.*"

"Goodnight Papa."

Mr. White

Dinner is to be served at seven-thirty, with drinks at seven. The entire staff is abuzz of the affair and the likely outcome. If I was keen on listening into office gossip, I'd be putting my money on Esme. The woman has fire in the eyes.

I pass a late lunch spread, leftovers from a diplomatic meeting between Moncleve and an unknown official, in the dining room. My stomach growls at the smell of smoked ham and deviled eggs and I appease it with a stick of gum. I'm on the job and even the slightest misstep could mean a mistake. And I don't make them.

Whistling under my breath, I roll the sterling silver cart, loaded with cleaning supplies, trash bags, and fresh flowers, to the servant's elevator. A little efficient thing, big enough for one person and the cart. I reach the fourth floor of the west wing and roll it down the length of the rich upholstered hallway. Moncleve does at least have taste. I stop at a large copy of a Monet above a pearl table filled with roses, I have the sensation of being watched.

Zachariah Moncleve is fastening a pair of gold cufflinks. I smile, rather than grab the blade in my breast pocket.

"Good afternoon. You're new."

So, the man pays attention to his staff. A possible complication, but unlikely.

"Yes, Barry White." I answer with a formal nod. I've gone under so many names, it's a wonder I haven't confused them. "I was hired last month."

"And you like your position in the staff?"

I smile politely, smoothing my freshly ironed suit. The dove gray compliments my dark features. "Oh yes. You have a lovely home. Art trades must be a lucrative business."

It may be too much, but I can't help toeing the line. Or I wouldn't be in this business at all. Moncleve is warm and it loosens the knot in my stomach. The reports said he was well-liked. I can see why. It's a shame I'm here to snatch right from under his nose, or we likely would have gotten along.

"That it is. Listen, I've a favor to ask. Will you do something for me?"

"Of course." Better not be too timely. I've a schedule to keep.

He goes into his room, and returns with a bottle of Macallan single malt. I recognize the year.

"This is good scotch."

"Indeed. I'd like you to put this in Dayton Jepsen's room. Do you know which one it is?"

"I clean it every other day."

"Good. Place it somewhere visible, beside these."

He reaches into his jacket and withdraws a thick Cuban cigar with a heavy envelope. I accept them. Inside, I am doing handstands.

"Celebrating something?"

Moncleve's smile is disarming. "I certainly hope so. If the man has any sense, we will be. Please get these to his room when he leaves for dinner. I don't want them to be seen beforehand."

I nod, offer my warmest grin, drape a dishtowel over the scotch, cigar, and note. Without another glance at him, I leave and enter the first bedroom. In an hour, I'll be in Jepsen's room.

And when I am, I've been given an even better opportunity than I could have hoped for. I might as well be paying Moncleve to do the job for me. I arrange hydrangeas on an antique dresser. "No." I laugh quietly. "I'm not that chivalrous."

Chapter 17   *A Dream is a Wish the Heart* Makes

Dayton

"So we've got our way in."

Jacob Benson, the primary on the La Grande Caccia operation, sits opposite me warming a neat bourbon between his hands. "Kristian confirmed this morning. He will be in place at the night of the ball."

Jacque sighs and the sound is short-tempered. "Kristian Johansen has been working for Molin for upwards of fifteen years. How is he to be trusted?"

"Because he's been wanting a way out of the Condors for the last ten of those. This is the best way to secure a safety net for his family so he can retire at once."

I nod slowly. "It's as good a deal as we could have hoped for. With operatives outside the building as backup and a man inside, we can take the entire manor down and ensure the Tormina family goes with it."

"Have all of Molin's guests RSVP'd?"

Benson smirks. "Of course they did. It's the highlight of the year for the Condor syndicate. Not a one of those Danes is going to be caught dead away from it."

"No offense intended."

"None taken."

Jacque's expression is accepting. "We've received

all of the shipments and are fully stocked. I'll be pulling Mendez, Collins, and Chekov for the crew. Benson, I want you as lead. And Jepsen, you will remain with me at the van."

Though I suspected this, I try not to react to being put on the back burner. "I'll do my best to play nice."

"Good. We wouldn't want a temper tantrum to interfere."

Benson looks at me but we don't say anything. It's water under the bridge. We've already gone over how close I am to this and how I can't see the job with the third party detachment of a Phantom. I'm tempted to discuss Esme with Benson and his involvement . . . but I refrain.

Benson stands, closes his folder, and checks his Timex. "We're finished here. I believe Jacque and I have a date with our ordinance specialist. And Dayton, you have one with Esme?"

I follow Benson as he leaves. "I've just enough time to put on a suit."

"You'll be needing flowers."

"What?"

"Flowers. If you expect to woo a woman, always bring flowers. Especially with a woman so beautiful."

They leave me standing in the Prep room with files, a pen, and a scowl. I'm aware of the household's interest in me and Esme. We haven't exactly worked to keep it a secret. But this is the fourth person today, who has suggested, or rather, told me I will need all the help I can get. As if I have little chance of garnering the lady without the trappings of flowers or wine or . . . chocolate.

Am I sweating like some pubescent teen over this dinner?

Stalking out of the room like a panther for the kill, I ignore the staff or other Phantoms and seclude myself in my own room. Here, I calm the unease. I choose a dark gray suit, with white shirt and skip the tie. I don't think it's needed between us tonight. Not for the informal statement of love I'm planning on giving.

Leaving my room before seven, I take the stairs in the alcove at the end of the hall nearest Esme's room and head to the roof.

I see Esme standing in a wash of breezy peach and apricot tones.

Her hair is loosely tied into a bun, pieces of it tangle over her cheeks and neck. Her flamingo pink dress snugs over every curve as if created on her. My mouth is completely dry and if she doesn't say something first, I'm going to croak out a greeting and embarrass myself.

"Hello."

"Hello." Just friends with this woman? Not a chance.

"I went ahead and asked for watermelon spritzers, in honor of our first shared drink on the island."

I get my voice back. "The island seems so far away."

I reach for Esme's hand and she entwines her fingers with mine. It bolsters my reserves. What's between us is right. It's that simple and that complicated. I have to believe Esme feels the same.

"It does."

She hands me my glass. We enjoy the drink with a view of Madrid. It's the first semblance of peace I've known in five days. And for once, it's with another person. It is not the first time I marvel at her ability to quell the demons within me.

"You look very beautiful tonight."

Esme grins without looking at me. "And you look debonair. Are you planning something special for tonight?"

"Maybe."

She faces me. Those blue eyes delve into me. I suspect she already knows.

"It should make things interesting. Dinner is here."

Two servers arrive with a fragrant meal. From a culinary standpoint, I cannot help but be impressed with the aesthetics as well as the choice of food. Huevos Rotos has always been a favored dish of mine when in Spain. By the aroma it's been done perfectly. I will have to thank Hernandez when I stop in the kitchens.

"Gracias."

The dark man cleans the edges of the plates and says happily, *"Eres muy bienvenidos."*

Esme and I sit at a little table overlooking the city. Even as the sun is dropping beneath the horizon, the life of Madrid never ends.

"It's very good."

"Yes, Hernandez always cooks well. I've learned quite a few things from him."

"You know everyone by name, including the staff."

"I try to make a habit of learning names. It's a part of the job."

"And you . . . you don't like people. But you try to. That's admirable."

"I wouldn't say I try to. But it comes off better if I appear civil when speaking to the people who cook my meals and clean my clothes. You know what I mean?"

Esme grins, and takes another bite. "I like Spain. It's warm. Rich with color. It makes me feel so alive."

I am caught up in her expression. "I suppose it does."

"Have you been terribly busy today? You look a little tired, Dayton."

Though her concern is real, Esme seems to be struggling to fit herself into the mold of a woman moving on from a past relationship. It fills me with relief.

"It's been a long week. But the next promises to be

a better one."

"Does it?" Esme sips her drink and watches me.

I can sense her desire to ask about the Hunt Ball. To know the details. If it isn't that tonight has a near magical quality to it and I plan on spilling my guts shortly. I would humor her. As it is, I need to remain focused on the objective at hand—to keep calm, and tell Esme she's the first woman I've ever loved.

I pray I won't be sick.

"Mmmm, and how about you Esme? Have fun shopping yesterday? Find that perfect something you've been searching for?"

Her expression is all innocence. "I had a much needed manicure actually. I've treated my nails terribly in the last weeks."

We eat, exchange polite chit-chat. I play along until the muscles of my jaw ache from grinding my teeth.

"How long do you plan on pretending with me tonight Esme? How long are you going to play?"

Her expression changes, eyes so blue they resemble a deep lake. The certainty falls into place. The fear of rejection fades at the realization this might be my only chance to set things straight between us. I will say what needs to be said and then whatever will happen, must happen.

Esme

"Am I pretending Dayton?"

"Isn't that what you've been doing these last days? Pretending . . . punishing."

"I've not been punishing you." The first stirrings of fear come. There is a distinct possibility my gamble has done harm, not good.

"No?"

"No. I've been busy." *Plotting, flouncing . . . doing my best to drive you mad.* "Living and moving on."

Dayton stands quickly. "How can you say that to me? First you want to know how I feel about us and now . . . you're moving on?"

My cover is blown. It's time to show my cards and pray everything pans out.

"What choice did I have? You said you wanted to keep things simple. Unattached."

"I never said unattached. Don't put words in my mouth, Esme."

"Okay fine. You hinted at it. You might as well have said it. I felt something completely different than you. I didn't want to get myself further involved with a man who doesn't want me."

"You might have given me more time. I've never experienced anything in my life like this . . . sharing feelings, emotion—it doesn't come easy for me. I didn't handle it well. I didn't know what to do."

"No." But I can see maybe I didn't either.

"I never said I didn't want you, Esme."

Truth. I can hear it in his voice—it's a balm for my wounds. I close my eyes, and clasp my hands beneath the table.

"It didn't seem like it at the time. It hurt me. Badly."

"I'm sorry."

Rough fingers brush over my cheek. I open my eyes. Dayton isn't standing at the other side of the table. He's kneeling in front of me, face close, eyes searching.

"Why did you run from me, Esme?"

My voice is weak. "I didn't run." But I'm afraid he'll see the truth. "I was hiding."

"From me?"

"Yes, Dayton. You. I looked at you, all of you, and I've never wanted more. I like your pride, even your arrogance. The dry humor you try to hide and the way you'll slow everything, just so you might cook a meal."

In too deep to back out now, I throw my hands up.

"Hell, I even fell for how you like to drink your coffee before speaking to me in the morning. You can't imagine what I felt. What I'm—"

"I can." His hand touches my neck—the back of it.

His warmth closes me in. I don't fight it.

"Because I'm in love with you, Esme.

My hands clutch his shirt. "What?"

"Esme, I love you. And I am in love with you. I love your laugh, the way it lights your face. Your depth of character to the point you don't see bad when you should. I love your love of fashion, and the way you create with it. I even love those abnormal furry slippers you adore, because every time I think of them, I see you. I see you in everything. Esme."

Dayton's hand squeezes my neck, his eyes so rich they shouldn't be real. "I . . . I love you. All of you."

"Oh my God."

"Yes, my sentiments exactly."

I shake my head. "Are you sure?"

"Yes, but becoming less so as you've yet to say the crucial response."

"Oh." I smooth my hands on his chest. "Oh, Dayton. I love you . . . you can't imagine how very much I do."

For those who say time does not stop for true love's kiss, they are wrong. Because it most certainly does. Especially for a woman like me. I have the heart of a true corny romantic.

That so-often-angry mouth crushes mine, his lips unyielding and firm. I take the pressure and the heat, my insides turn to molten lava as my heart leaps into ecstasy.

This, with arms tight and heart pressed to heart, is how lovers are made. It's how sacred bonds are forged for life. In this kiss, this singeing, demanding kiss, I can see our future folding outward. And with it, a love that will burn away the darkest of days.

When the kiss grows urgent and desperate, Dayton carefully pulls himself back and a great part of me is disappointed as he does, even as I understand it. Even as I love him for it.

As is becoming habit, he rests his forehead on mine.

Dayton smiles. "I do believe, this is how it's supposed to go."

"I think so. But if you think it's not proper, we can—"

Dayton's mouth teases mine. "You know if I keep kissing you, this will end on the rooftop, right here, right now."

My stomach pitches. Excitement and laughter. "Yes."

"I don't want it to be blind passion. You're the first woman I've ever loved, Esme. And God-willing, you'll be the last. Aside from any moral objections to taking advantage of the situation, I want the first time we are together to be private, planned, and free of Carl's ghost."

I cringe at the name in conjunction with Dayton and my skin ripples with gooseflesh. I wish I never have to hear that name again. "I don't want him in our bed."

Dayton's hands are warm on my arms. Reassuring. "And he won't be. After next week, it will just be us. And we can take time to know each other better." His eyes are promising. "On every level. If that's what you want."

I laugh. It lightens the mood. "It's what I want. Though I'll warn you now, I'll do my best to drive you to the edge of sanity. Not that I won't also drive myself mad in the process . . . then there's Zach. He'll want this to be done properly. He'll want us to be married first."

Dayton groans as I run my fingers through his hair

and kiss him soundly, despite my strung out list of objections.

He catches my hips in his hands and presses his face into my neck. "I've changed my mind. Right here. Right now."

Giggling now, I pull away from his mouth and shake my finger at him. "You will remember, when the lust fades, how you wanted things and you'll be happier for it—so will I."

"Maybe. Maybe not."

"We'd better go to bed then."

Dayton's eyes travel the length of me and I think my clothes might smolder off.

"Separately."

"As you wish." He says with mocking eyes.

"If that's a Princess Bride reference then I know we are soulmates."

Dayton grins. "Soulmates, *mijn zoete*. Get some sleep for us both. I doubt I'll sleep a wink after this."

Laughing, heart full, I watch Dayton head to the roof access, his shoulders are strong. In the glow of twinkle lights surely this is a dream. The best dream of my life.

Dayton looks over his shoulder, offering me a wolfish grin as a goodnight. I blow him a kiss like a besotted princess at a window. Dayton Jepsen loves me and we're going to live happily ever after.

After we kill the very bad king and all of his horsemen.

Chapter 18 *Love Hurts*

Dayton

"Nice." I'm smiling as I lay the congratulatory note on the balcony and swirl scotch in my glass. Courtesy of Zach, I'm enjoying a twenty-year old bottle of single malt liquor and a very fat, very tasty Cuban cigar.

This night, couldn't get better. Unless of course, I'd decided to lose all sense of romance and storm Esme's door to finish what we started on the roof. The idea is too tempting, so I take two slugs of scotch and let my mind wander instead.

To a life made with Esme Moncleve, or . . . I frown trying to recall the surname she'd gone with most of her life and fail. It's something with a C. Coris? Camella? I suppose it doesn't matter. I'll ask her another day. Now that I'm reconciled to loving, I want to know everything about her. The invisible chains which prevented me from asking more of her—demanding really, are gone. I'd been afraid of connecting myself so thoroughly to another person, particularly one of the opposite sex because I didn't think I could give anyone my life.

Now, warmed from the scotch, I think I never had a choice on the matter. Whatever you'd like to call it, fate, or as Zach says—God designed it so I would meet and love

Esme. I never had a chance.

I'm certainly glad of it. All's well, that ends well.

After a while longer, I finish the scotch. It must be later than I thought or I've underestimated my ability to hold liquor. I can hardly see straight. Frowning, I stumble awkwardly off the small balcony and back into the murky confines of my bedroom. In here, my disorientation becomes overwhelming and I fall face first after catching a shoe on the large area rug beneath the four-poster bed.

Shaking my head, growing disconcerted—and angrier by the second at the effect the alcohol has on me, I hardly notice when a lanky figure materializes beside me.

"Have no fear Jepsen. I won't be the one to kill you."

I recoil at the unfamiliar voice, clear of any accent. It feels like I'm pinned by lead in each limb. The most I can manage is a weak roll onto my back, so I can see my attacker, and my eyes make three copies of him.

"What . . . do . . . you want?" My voice sounds alien and I struggle to run through the inventory of poisons I am accustomed to ingesting. Their side effects and survivability.

"I don't want anything to do with you actually. I'm here, strictly on business."

I stare up at him, eyes wanting to close, fighting the invisible but belligerent fatigue.

He comes close enough I can make out a blade straight nose and very dark eyes. Even if I wanted to, I couldn't see any other defining characteristics. Most especially as it is two noses and four sets of eyes I'm examining.

"Molin," I whisper. My mouth helplessly dry, I taste the sedative now. Some sort of barbiturate. Likely Amytal or Pentothal.

"Bingo. I should have given you a larger dose. I'd like you to be out faster than this."

He says it with detached study, he grabs my chin and shakes my head from side to side.

I grit my teeth. "*Varken.*"

Pig. It doesn't matter I say it in Dutch, I'm certain he hears me.

It is the last thing I say to my captor. My last image however, is of a lean face glaring at me with a grim smile and a sigh of acceptance. Strange, I think he agreed with me.

Esme

"We've been looking for forty-eight hours! Something is wrong."

"We don't know that."

"I know it. I can feel it, Papa."

Zachariah and Adrienne exchange a look of concern as though I'm a mental patient near the point where I scream obscenities whilst tossing furniture. I rarely reach the Hulk level, but I am deadly close to doing it now. They can't understand what I'm feeling firsthand, I've tried to convey the message with urgency. It should not have been missed after so many hours of attempting it. They should be as anxious to resolve this as I am. And damn it, they should believe me when I say something is terribly wrong!

"He's done it before, Esme. It is very likely to be the case again."

I'm desperate. "He would have told me. We said we loved each other the last night I saw him. He wouldn't say something like that and then run. What would be the point?"

"He may not have had time to explain." Adrienne's voice is soft and gentle. It makes me want to weep. Dayton didn't run away. Not after saying he loved me. I know it. This is bigger than simply not remembering to leave a stupid note.

"Either he is hurt somewhere or stranded. I refused to believe otherwise."

Zach stands and sighs. "I hope you're right. Because if you're not, I'm going to tear that boy limb from limb when he shows his face."

The threat does little to help my fast-fleeting control.

Our impromptu meeting is interrupted by a knock at the study door. Zach cracks it open and speaks in low tones with the mansion's head of security, Bartholomew. Everyone calls him Bart. His military short hair contrasts with his gentle eyes. Apparently he's fond of the goatee business. Benson said it's because he doesn't like his cleft chin . . . wants to cover it.

My mind is even rambling.

Zach comes back with a small box, unmarked and sealed.

"What is it?"

"There was a package delivered here an hour ago. Security has already scanned for explosives. There is nothing harmful in nature within, so it's safe to open. But the box is unmarked."

"You think it's to do with Dayton?" Adrienne says with a hollow tone.

My voice comes out choked. "What? Why about Dayton?"

Rather than answer us, Zach takes the box, settles in the chair at his desk. And with a sleek knife, carefully slices the seals on the four sides. He lifts the lid as if a most fragile substance. His stare is intense.

"What's inside?" Adrienne asks politely.

I strain to hear the answer.

His eyes are locked on the contents, face suddenly bone white. All that comes from him, is a whispered, "*Mon Dieu!*"

"What?"

I want to know, I need to know.

Adrienne and I move next to him. What awaits us is surreal. My stomach rolls with horror. I cover my mouth and stare, unable to look away from a small plastic bag containing a human toe. Beneath it, a hank of dirty blond hair and a slip of paper. I know with sickening clarity the identity of the owner as well as the sender . . . and I must sit on the floor—or collapse.

"Dayton. Oh my God, they have Dayton."

"Esme, take a deep breath." Zach is kneeling beside me, but all I can see is Dayton's toe in a box with a chunk of his hair. They packaged his toe like a piece of meat for our viewing pleasure. Sickness floods me and threatens to send me into violent heaving.

He can't be dead.

There is a low keening sound and it takes several seconds of hearing it to realize it's me. Rocking, I try to focus on Zach. I've fallen. I'm struggling, I have to fight with all my strength to win. After several minutes I get up. When I do, I'm trembling in his arms—ice cold.

"How did this happen?"

"I do not know. I will find out. Esme. Breathe."

"I'm trying."

The room stops spinning and rage grows beyond terror. I am desperate not to sink. I can't be of any help if I'm lost in fear.

I wipe my face. "A note?"

"*Oui.*"

"I want to read it."

"That doesn't matter now. I will take care of everything. I want you to rest now."

Zach's voice is soothing like a father's should be with enough command to have me consider it.

"No."

"Esme, please, listen. You haven't slept in two days and you must sleep. You're still in shock."

"Stop it." I pull away from his arms so I can see the room clearly. Adrienne is gone. We are alone. I'm grateful for it. "I want to read the note. I'm not going to fall apart."

"It's in Dutch."

"Then you can translate."

Our eyes lock in a war of wills and I know without a doubt where my stubborn streak comes from. "*Oui.* I can translate. But it will not help you."

"I'll be the judge of that."

Zach steadies me and I am relieved the box, as well as its contents, has been taken from the room. A square of folded parchment is open on the wood. I stare at it, thinking somehow this piece of paper will lead to Dayton appearing in front of me. But I know that's impossible.

"Read it. Please." The anger is the only comfort I have at present. I do my best to use it rather than let it rule me.

Picking up the letter, Zach's jaw works several times as he scans it—his face colorless.

'You will recognize the little gifts we sent as a sign of Dayton Jepsen's capture. This, above all else, is what I wish you to keep in mind when you make your move.'

Zach stops. He eyes me.

"Please. Go on. I need to hear it."

'We have been playing this game for weeks and now, I have finally gained the upper hand. Do not think I won't use it at any cost. I am more ruthless than that of my son, and you, Esme, will know that better than anyone.'

He frowns, his eyes filled with fury.

'You knew I would come for you. And though I failed the first time, I learned my lesson. I no longer need to come for you. Because you, are going to come to me. I will be expecting your presence at the La Grande Caccia ball. You are well aware of this get together and will remember it requires formal dress. There, I will meet you and we may discuss further what it is, I plan on doing to you and of

course, your lover. Do not think I am unaware of your attachment to him. It is this attachment I am counting on, to secure your cooperation. If you do not come, if you fail to have the fortitude to save him, then I will kill him at once. And resume my hunt for you until either your corpse is in my hands, or you are brought to me whole and living. You can imagine what I will have in mind for you at that point in time.

You have failed to remember the family which you wronged. I will make sure you never forget. Be at the Ball and don't bring any of your new babysitters. I will have no trouble removing Jepsen's head rather than his toe.

"He did not sign his name."

"Coward." My hands are fists, my teeth grind so tight there's pain

"*Oui. La pire espèce.*"

A world of words flows between my father and me without speaking. We understand each other but that doesn't mean this will be any easier because of it.

"I have to."

"No. You don't. He will kill you both."

"I have to try. I can't leave him."

"Esme, he would not want this. Dayton would try to stop you."

"And he would fail. Just like you are. You can't stop me. I have to do this because I love him. You should understand this better than anyone Papa. You love him too."

"He is a son to me."

Zach's eyes tighten, as if to keep feelings from exposing themselves.

"And I am your daughter, but I need him." My heart hurts under the stark reality of losing Dayton to Molin. I can't imagine it. It's too close to the reality. "I'm going to that ball. And you're going to kill Molin."

Zach's emotion leaves as quickly. "I'm going to annihilate him—all of them."

"Yes, I'm counting on it."

Chapter 19 *Get Going or Get Gone*

Esme

I'm in the gym by five in the morning, running on the treadmill with a deadly focus. Having been up most of the night, plagued with nightmares new and old, I figured the gym is better than lying awake imagining what Molin could be doing to Dayton.

As I stop at the four-mile mark, I notice Benson beside me. Sawing breath, my heart thundering in my ears.

"Fancy seeing you here. Did Zach send you?"

"It doesn't matter if he did. I would have wanted to come."

"Mmmm." I grab the towel and sponge my neck and face. "I'm going to the ball. He can't stop me."

"Actually, he could. But I don't think he's going to try. You're just like him. You'd find a way."

"Damn right." Pleased with Benson acquiescing, I move to the weights and pick out a pair of ambitious ten-pounders for my reps.

"You're angry."

I lift the weights, press up, then lower and repeat. "Yes."

"It will help you train harder. Sometimes a good

thing."

I lift three reps. "Sometimes not?"

"It depends, are you stronger doing this? Better focused?" Benson's eyes are unflinching as he studies me.

I don't hesitate. "Yes. It's something I can control. I can be ready for him . . . like in some small way, I'm doing everything I possibly can to save the man I love. And kill the men who tried to take him from me."

Benson's laugh is warm and eases the tension.

"Then it's good for you. Within reason. If you overdo it, the only thing you will accomplish is to exhaust yourself physically before the real battle has even begun. And I need you in top shape for this mission."

"This mission . . ." I stop, resting the weights on my thighs as I sit on the bench.

Benson sits opposite me. "Since you're going to be at the ball no matter what anyone has to say about it, I've decided it's better to work with you—than possibly against you."

"You're letting me in."

"Yes. I'm letting you in. We have four days till La Caccia Grande and by midnight of the night in question, I intend to finish things the way God intended. With a bang."

I lean forward, eye to eye with Benson. "I can't bring anyone. Molin said he'll kill Dayton on the spot if he saw anyone."

"You won't be bringing anyone . . . on the inside. We have a contact in Molin's ranks who is attending that evening. This contact has been given explosives—he has already placed on the main supports of the structure. With our help on the outside, you won't have to go alone."

"But I will be alone with Molin." I don't realize how scared I sound until Benson's hand grasps my own, to encourage me.

"Until you have eyes on Dayton, yes. You will be alone. It's going to be close. And there is a distinct possibility the bomb may go off with you inside. But right now the chance of that is small. I plan on making that chance a zero. We should be able to get you in, get Dayton, and out before midnight. I'm warning you now, if Dayton isn't with you when I come, I'll be taking you regardless."

"Can't someone wait till we're out?"

Benson shakes his head. "The explosives are set on a timer so no person needs to be in close proximity when the time comes. Unfortunately, it means you will be on a time crunch. But I doubt Molin will wait long to take you to Dayton. He'll want to start immediately."

"With torturing us."

"You, yes. He's most likely having fun with Dayton as we speak."

I stare at Benson. "I suppose I should be grateful you don't pull any punches."

"Yes. You should be prepared for the worst."

"Gee thanks."

Benson's smile contrasts with our stark conversation.

"You're tough." He slaps his hand to my arm making the skin sting, and squeezes it in a brotherly grip. "I'll take care of you. Focus on keeping yourself alive and Molin unaware. I'll do the rest."

"I wish that were comforting."

"Me too, but hey, can't have everything we want. Saddle up."

Benson stands, rolling his neck, shaking his arms to loosen the tightness. When I remain seated in a patient sort of way, he crooks his finger beckoning me.

"Until Saturday, we work. Everyday. I want as much defensive and offensive training in you as possible. One can never be too prepared."

"Does my father brand that into every one of your skulls?"

I get up, rolling my own neck as I contemplate what

Benson might throw at me. He's already crouching, his eyes narrowing on my hips and feet. Something he's drilled into me before. Movement always comes from the belly button first. Watch that, see the movement and anticipate.

"Focus, Esme. Dayton depends on it."

Dayton

The sound of faint music playing above my head wakes me from a fitful sleep. And my eyes crack into slits to take in the dim lighting of the room. Lying on my side, I study the room in grey-scale, allowing my body to feel the pain it wants. Then I work to control that response.

I've been here for three days. And by here, I am under no illusions as to my location or of my captors' identities. The walls are stucco white, the floor pale cement, and if I focus well enough, I smell a touch of jasmine in the air from the slats of thin rectangular windows that hug the ceiling. Jasmine bushes are at the base of the building. I am in the basement of the Tormina estate.

If the familiarity of my surroundings were not enough to solidify this, the men's voices, heavy with Dutch, is a clue.

Sitting up, I regulate my breathing to settle the sensation of queasiness. I assess the state of my health, as I have every morning, and for the most part, I am in a functional capacity. My hands and wrists are swollen from repeated binding, as are my ankles. My face is sore, bruised, in several places, but without any fractures and I am grateful for that.

Aside from a likely rib fracture and my most frustrating injury, a missing toe, I am able to move with manageable pain. As for my mental state, I volley between reckless blood-red rage and subdued thoughtfulness. I think of Esme as little as possible. Because she is a distraction and one I cannot afford if I am going to escape.

Molin has a plan. But I don't intend to be part of it. I've already succeeded in singling out the weakest of foot soldiers, and I've deduced, my best course will be to wait until the night of the La Caccia Grande to act. Molin will suspect something then, which could hamper my chances, but it is likely the need for extra security for the ball will strain his resources, and give me a covered exit. Subduing the one night guard should not be a problem, nor should bypassing the security on the open grounds of the courtyard. The Amstel will be a welcome avenue of escape once I reach its waters at the outer perimeter of the Tormina property.

I can't think of Esme's part in this. Or how Molin will try to incorporate her. Because she is most certainly at the center of it, though I doubt Molin is doing anything less than shouting for joy over my capture. I expected a visit from the doddering badger by now.

"Are you sleeping in?" The voice is young, mocking, and who I've been spending my time thinking about—the weak link in the chain.

Albert is smiling at me from the metal doorway. With broad shoulders, narrow hips, and a face close to skeletal, the youth he exudes is unmistakable, as is his desire to impress Molin. I was like him once. It's a pity I'll be forced to kill, or if he is fortunate, only severely wound him.

"Good morning." My voice light and the language Dutch. It gives us common ground.

"I've brought you some breakfast."

"Any bacon?"

He scoffs, but there is amusement there and I lift my chin as we share smiles. "I'm afraid it is oats again."

"Too bad." I accept the bowl and carefully spoon a

bite into my mouth. Several of my teeth are loose and I don't want to risk swallowing one.

"What does he have planned for me today, Albert? Anything special?" The use of the boy's first name is no mistake. It denotes a personal relationship or at least that we aren't really at odds. Something I want Albert to be thinking about.

Albert raises his golden brows, his eyes intent mine. "I don't believe so. I do think he might be dropping by for a visit late this afternoon."

"Molin wants to see me?"

"That is the rumor."

"I'll be pleased to entertain him. Although my humble abode is lacking his usual taste."

Albert chuckles. "You are remarkably funny for a dead man."

"Dead men are always funnier."

I meekly grin over the bowl. He may construe that however he likes.

"You must be important to Molin to be watching after me so carefully."

"I am very important to him. I was initiated into the Condors at seventeen. That's unheard of."

I agree. "Young. You must be something then."

"I heard you were a coward during your initiation. You choked and then deserted."

I finish my oats. "You heard correctly. I found other pursuits to be more diverting . . . and profitable."

"Being a Condor is of the highest profit."

"Emotionally. Money-wise? I found being my own boss to be better all around. But what do I know? I'm the one sitting on the floor of a basement waiting to be executed."

The smugness in Albert would be humorous if I didn't recognize it from my own early days. I'm looking in a mirror from a dozen years ago, a disconcerting and unwelcome vision.

"I'll be just outside if you need something. If you do, don't count on getting it. You know where the piss pot is."

I glance over to the pot. "I'm very familiar with it now. Thanks."

When the door squeaks closed, I sag into the stucco at my back. I drift into myself for a time, calculating risks and scenarios until the sunlight leaking through window slats changes morning to afternoon.

Then he comes, as prophesied.

As though I am on the other end of a thread to Molin, I sense him before I see him. This gives me the time needed to struggle into a stand so I can view him eye to eye. And it is indeed a struggle. The door swings open and he enters. I don't see the guards outside the doorway, but I know they are near.

The years have not changed him, other than a thickening waistline. His silver hair cut military-short highlights a pair of milky blue eyes. The wrinkles have deepened, and his eyes are severe, but Molin is Molin. A cantankerous prig of a crime Lord.

"Well, well. It has been a long time Dayton. You've grown up."

I smirk. "A little. Twelve years will do that to a man. How's the family business treating you?"

"Good. I have no trouble paying the bills. As you already know. His grin is sinister and amusement ripples in his clouded eyes. "So tell me, did you ever think to see me again?"

"No." My answer is honest.

Molin works his way further into the room, leaving the door open—his eyes roving over the floor. It's hard for me not to lunge at him.

"I must admit, for a time, I thought Moncleve killed

you. I felt it a terrible shame."

"Did you?"

"Maybe not. Hindsight is twenty-twenty. If I knew you were going to defect and become one of Moncleve's best, I might have tried harder to retain you. But, what's done is done."

"Not quite."

"Ah, you refer to Esme Moncleve now."

My jaw flexes. I must remain in control. Always in control.

"No need to pretend. I already know all about your lusty affair. The staff waggle their tongues enough. But that isn't the point. There is no use in trying to protect Esme's reputation . . . as we have been careful to avoid any mistakes."

"What is the point, then?"

He raises his eyebrows. "Haven't you already guessed it? You are my bargaining chip. I have no need to chase any longer. Because I hold the ace. She will come for you and when she does, this frivolous little game will be over."

The blood drains from my face. For all my feigned strength, I am so lightheaded I lean into the wall for support. It is not missed by Molin. I have nothing but hatred for him.

Somewhere in my calculation, and 'interrogative' sessions, I thought of this. But hearing it, knowing I've already played my part in possibly hurting Esme—makes me sick.

"Coward."

"Debatable, Dayton. Yet even you must see the genius in this."

My eyes burn into him. "I will end you."

"You will try. But I don't see how that is possible from inside these walls, hmmm?" He gestures around the room, then points to my missing toe. "Especially as you are a gimp now."

Laughter comes up. If he thinks that will be a barrier to my killing him, then Molin has lost brain cells where he gained fat.

"Something funny?"

"Yes."

"Do tell Dayton. I am in need of a laugh."

I recline further into the wall, forcing the muscles in my torso to relax. "I won't need to tell you, you'll know."

Molin makes a sound of disgust. "My God, you're just the same. A bratty kid with an ego the size of a whale."

I force a confident smile.

"I hope you wear that smile right up until I gut you. It will make sensational photos for the Tribune Chronicle when your body washes up in the Amstel.

Albert, keep your eyes on him. I don't want Jepsen to sneeze without someone noticing. And send for Bram. I think we're in need of a tune up. But don't let him take anything else . . . just make sure it's a good reminder of who's in control."

"I've been missing Bram. Two days is far too long between visits."

"Hmm, I'm sure he'll feel the same. I hear he was positively gushing about your last one. Little toes tend to get rather exciting at the dinner table."

My stomach cramps. "I love to entertain." And I keep my deliberate smile.

Molin waves a hand to dismiss me, and heads for the door. When he leaves, the metal frame groans back into place, and I do the same—with fatigue, frustration and anger. I sink to the floor. "Damn him."

Running my hands through my hair, I slip back, piece by frayed piece into myself until

all I can think of is the mission. It must be my focus.

Dear God, I don't speak with you often, but keep

Esme from coming here.

Chapter 20 *Guardian in Distress*

Esme

The air is brusque, and scented with roses and jasmine. The sky, a fading purple bruise touched with fingers of sunlight. I stop in the oval driveway of the Tormina manor, filled with sleek black vehicles and smartly dressed Dutch patrons. My stomach rebels at the familiar sight and I tell myself not to panic. I can do this. I must do this.

"*Bent u Nou, missen?*"

I turn. The tuxedo-clad valet is staring at me.

"I'm sorry. I only speak English."

"That is no problem. Are you all right?"

"Yes, of course . . . the manor. It's stunning at twilight. Molin has outdone himself."

He gives a cursory glance of the building, then smiles obligingly. "Absolutely. Have a good evening, miss"

"Thank you." I step around him and follow the small crowd of guests. It's like drowning in formal gowns. Everywhere there is another face, another dress. Another tuxedo and sharp jawline. Another soul who belongs to Tormina and everything he entails.

I stride toward the ballroom—my brilliant garnet silk gown swishing about my ankles.

I decided to wear it with large sparkling diamonds, courtesy of my father. Now, standing in a room filled with exquisiteness, I am glad for my choice as it makes me appear not only exclusive and highbrow, but it easily singles me out for Molin. I want there to be no mistake that I intend to face him out in the open.

"You look incredible, Esme."

I turn, eyes lighting on a man who I vaguely remember as Molin's favorite. I forget his name, I've met him on several occasions. By the glint in his obsidian eyes, he is fully aware of the circumstances of my return to the manor. And yet, he is so friendly and kind. I wish I didn't know better.

"Thank you."

"Would you care for a drink?" He asks softly.

"No. I'd like to see Molin."

"He will be busy entertaining guests for a time. The La Grande Caccia is the Condor's biggest event."

The gloss of the other guests is dulled because I know who, and what they are. I was so young and foolish when I met Carl. This ball was once like a fairy tale. Now, the darkness oozes beneath the shine and it resembles a horror film.

"I came for Dayton."

"And you'll see him when Molin wants you to." I strive for patience as it could quite literally mean life or death. "Yes, of course." I survey the room with practiced boredom. "I'm sure I'll find a way to busy myself until then."

"Wonderful. Don't be a stranger. I'll be happy to dance with you if you don't have a partner."

The idea of dancing with Molin's lead puppet makes me shudder internally. But didn't I willingly dance the last two years with Carl, knowing full well what he was and what he did privately? I can't escape him here. He is everywhere.

Smiling tightly, I disappear into the crowd and mingle my way over to the wet bar on the far side of the ballroom. Men are pouring champagne in tall flutes and doling out whiskey in thick crystal. The liquid bubbles are too tempting to deny. Perhaps a little alcohol will stop the trembling in my hands.

I take a flute from the carved maple bar, then people-watch. On my side of the ballroom, I spot Molin laughing with another gentleman half his age, dressed the part of a wealthy gentleman.

The snake. Make that two snakes. Whoever that gentleman is, if he is laughing with Molin, he is equally guilty.

Fighting a shiver, I slowly sip champagne while moving in his general direction. I have agreed to play the game, there is no requirement I play by his rules alone. My time is too short to sit and idle whilst he finishes pleasing his favorite clients.

It takes me three dances, and two glasses of champagne, but I reach Molin and smile proudly. The fact that I can be so cordial with the father of the man I killed, who currently has the man I love as hostage—must be something to see. I know Dayton would be impressed, were he here to witness it.

"Good evening, Esme. You look lovely in that color."

I incline my head softly to Molin, but my tone is icy. "Where is Dayton? I don't want to be rude, but I've already spent a fair amount of time dancing and drinking. I think it's time to stop this façade. Don't you?" Brave words from a woman whose knees are knocking together beneath her dress.

"I forgot how much I liked you. What a pity how things turned out."

"Yes indeed. Where is Dayton?"

"Have you forgotten my son entirely then?"

My eyes are on Molin, my stomach knotting, as his scrutiny pierces me. He is as dead inside as his son. I don't know why I could never see it, until too late.

"There was nothing to forget by the end of us."

Silence is taut until a voice over my shoulder me shatters it.

"Nothing to forget? How very cruel of you, Esme."

I freeze, like being struck by a cattle prod. Before I can make my body turn, there is a familiar hand braced on the back of my neck. Breath, tinged with the smell of peppermint leaves and tobacco caresses my cheek, and my legs go weak.

It can't be him. I killed him.

"I've missed you." His voice burns into me. The weight of his hand hurts the nape of my neck

My breath rushes out in a gasp, and my vision clouds with terror. I'm hallucinating.

"I . . . I killed you."

The laughter shrouds me and when the hand allows me to turn, the same heavy pressure is on my shoulder and skirts my collarbone before slipping away, I'm staring at the deformed mask of Carl.

"My God. Carl, you're alive."

"No thanks to you . . . unfortunately."

Molin has said nothing at our reunion but I feel his interest in what happens next, like a wet-nose dog jabbing at my legs.

Carl's eyes are just the same, sharp as tacks in shades of navy. His face is a faint memory of what it used to be. Etched-in hard lines and puckered pink scarring, I can see how the bullet punctured his head, tearing into tissue. A hole in his cheek bone is ripe with scabbing and stomach-curdling crust. I'm shocked he is walking rather than lying in a bed—a vegetable.

"It's frightening, isn't it?"

"Carl . . . I'm—" I can hardly believe the first words I want to say are an apology. Forcing my mouth closed, I stare at his face and want to shrivel. His outsides, now match what is within. Such masculine beauty is always wasted on the man.

"Yes, I think we both know how you feel."

In a calculated motion his eyes assess my dress and figure. I grit my teeth.

"You came for Dayton."

It's clear Carl planned the actions this evening and is waiting for a triumphant opportunity to crush and maim his opponent. Or in this case, opponents. This is not the time to panic over Dayton's welfare. Or my own.

Carl's hands, eerily familiar, grip my shoulders. "I'm going to have a very good time tonight."

It is Molin's voice that floats over my head and responds. "Don't be at it all night, Carl. You have guests to attend to. And please, try to not to make too big of a mess."

My eyes flash to Carl's when he laughs, long and deep. His voice is tempered with victory. "Of course, Papa. I will not keep the guests waiting long. An hour . . . maybe two will suffice. Don't you think, Esme?"

I stare at him. My stomach is folding in on itself. It is 11:40 p.m. Benson will enter the premises in exactly ten minutes, then descend on wherever it is my tracker indicates. I'm ecstatically relieved he convinced me that the safest way was to swallow it. This morning, I thought the practice medieval. Now, there is little to be said of what I know about surviving . . . I know nothing. Carl will never know about the tracker, nor will he find it—safely ensconced in my digestive system. At least for a few hours.

But I will. And it will be enough. I will have time to get to Dayton and when we do, we will make it out of this. Everything will be fine.

It has to be.

Any other scenario has no place in my head, even as waves of dread are crashing there. I must stay focused or I might as well submit to defeat.

"Good evening then, Esme."

My eyes narrow and my mouth stiffens at the man who spawned Carl.

"Go to hell, Molin."

He laughs, a carbon copy of Carl's, then dismisses us with an impatient gesture. I don't even stumble trying to keep up with Carl's rigorous pace. I'm too anxious to leave the ballroom, the hundreds of questing eyes, and the sensation of being circled by vultures. Any place, will be better . . . particularly if it involves finding Dayton faster.

There is little time.

Sweat beads my forehead and neck, glistening like diamonds under the spray of LED lighting in the service hall. Carl is silent, his grip firm, and his jaw set. If I didn't understand him before, there is little doubt now how lost I will be. There is a part of him the bullet found which does not show. I sense that darkness in my companion as we walk side by side, through the Tormina manor, then descend deeper into her belly.

Here, the walls lose their delicate eggshell in favor of painted stucco. Plush carpeting, becomes echoing concrete underfoot.

"I never took you here."

I shake my head, ignoring the shiver that rushes my limbs and makes my hands go numb.

"I suppose I should have. I should have done many things actually."

An apology?

He stops at a huge steel door, reaching into a pocket for keys. When he lets go of my arm to open the door, there is a strong urge to run. Self-preservation, I suppose. I never understood how strong it could be. Until now. The only thing that stops me, is the prospect of leaving Dayton to the same fate as the Torminas.

I focus on this, until the door swings wide and my thoughts scatter like pearls from a broken necklace.

Dayton sits on a chair in the middle of the room, arms tied behind him, legs tied to each spindle. He sits erect and his eyes flutter open when the lights kick on at our entrance, it takes him several seconds to recognize me. When he does, his expression is bland. There is no warmth. No expression.

"Dayton!" I whisper. The frayed edges of Benson's voice cause me to tightly grip the little piece of metal in my hand.

Snorting, Carl shoves me into the room and I fall purposefully to my knees and into Dayton's lap. Our gazes meet for a brief blistering second. I give him a bone-breaking hug.

"That's enough."

I hold longer, inhale the scent of salt and blood on Dayton, working to maneuver the blade into one of his hands. A fist grabs my hair. Being drug by my hair is something, I am ashamed to say, I am acquainted with. That doesn't stop my yelp when I feel several strands are ripped out, as Carl tears me away from Dayton.

"You throw yourself at him like a whore."

Dayton's voice rumbles at my back.

"She's not a whore."

"Oh?" Carl steps around me, withdrawing a silken scarf from his tuxedo pocket to wipe his hands. "I suppose you'd know. You have been banging her the last few weeks. Or . . . well, I'm betting you've had your fill of her longer than that. Isn't that true Esme?"

"What?"

Carl turns, the light ripples over his puckered flesh.

"Did he help you decide to shoot me? Or was that little idea all of your own making?" He looks at Dayton. "I wouldn't put it past her, she's a real bitch when she chooses to be."

"Free me and we'll see who becomes the bitch."

Carl runs his tongue over his teeth. "Don't tempt me, Jepsen. I've got something planned and I don't want you to spoil things. Not when I've been wanting this so very badly."

"Then stop playing games, Carl." I taunt him, standing. I pray Dayton is working on his bindings. "Kill us both, or let us go."

Carl's eyes are lurid, his mouth wet. "My, my, you've grown, haven't you?"

I step back from Carl. If he sees me look toward Dayton, or notices the panic flaring within me, he doesn't show it. Rather, like a snake enchanted by a flute, he glides closer to me, his eyes never leaving mine.

I recognize the change in temperature, the dance of frightened prey stalked by the predator about a half a second in, then I bolt for the door.

As my hand closes over the handle, Carl slams into me from behind.

In scrabbling, stilted seconds, we battle for control, me clawing and hissing—Carl, laughing and clamping my body to his. Then everything, even my pulse, slows to a crawl.

I can hear Dayton's bellow of anger somewhere, very far away. With it, I am aware I've stopped screaming. Or was I screaming at all? I think I screamed . . . at first.

I've stopped moving.

The instinct to paralyze comes over me, and I am lifeless as Carl throws me to the ground with savage strength. My head knocks into the concrete, causing a chain reaction of fuzzy vision and desolate weakness to capture my limbs. A lamb for the slaughter, I can do nothing but stare up as Carl is above me, dragging me beneath him.

My dream was a premonition.

I saw Dayton and Carl together. And here they are.

Dayton, oh God, Dayton, is yelling for me. His voice sounds fearful, but too far away. Everything is far away.

Rough hands, dig into my skin, pulling and demanding. A mouth, contorted in rage grinds against mine, desperate for a response. Fabric tearing rends the air . . . and everything jumps into proper speed with sickening clarity. This jolts me from the sludge.

"No!" I grunt, fighting the hands now with savage determination. "No."

Carl's head jerks up from the crest of one breast, his face repulsive, and empty dead eyes.

"I'm going to kill you."

I buck up beneath him, squirming when his hands snap into place about my throat, completing his strangely poetic cycle. The scream is cut off when the air is.

The sensation of death, directly in front of me, staring into me and through me, is brief. One moment Carl is strangling me, his face red with rage and then, a pair of crimson-stained hands are on both sides of his face, as a loud sickening pop ends the struggle. Carl collapses on me in one heavy whoosh. I can't help the wail of panic that ensues when I scramble out from beneath the weight of a very dead Carl Tormina.

"*Esme, Schat. Ik ben hier. Ik ben hier Esme.*"

Dayton

"Esme, darling. I am here. I am here, Esme."

She is trembling violently, her skin like ice with pupils wide in shock. Against the backdrop of a lily-white face, one could easily mistake her for an extra on an undead drama series. As it is, I press her close, I forget her fragility, only to reassure myself of her safety.

She is whole. She is safe and whole.

When Carl's hands wrapped around her throat, terror climb into me with furious strength. I had shreds of rope still to cut. In a handful of seconds, I broke free from the chair crashing awkwardly to the floor with my ankles still bound as I crawled over to Esme. Her legs are jerking, arms like calcified branches, with Carl looming above her, playing his part as a reaper. There is nothing I could have done differently. On seeing the easiest opportunity, the most efficient method of eliminating the threat, I snapped Carl's neck in one clean break.

I don't see his body now, or notice the pieces of wood splintering into my legs.

I only see Esme. She's in my arms. Her scent is a breath of fresh air.

"I've missed you." My hoarse whisper disappears into her hair as I the first wave of relief is exchanged for exhaustion. It has been a great many long days.

"Dayton, my God, I was so worried."

She clings to me as strongly as I do her. The warmth of her tears settles me. A dead body lies a foot from my knees. A party continues above us, with a dull throb of music.

"Esme." I cup her face. Shock is there, she is sluggish and her thoughts seem distracted. "We need to leave. Fast!"

Her eyes widen.

"The bombs. Dayton." Terror lances through her voice. "The bombs are going to go off any minute."

Before I can say I know, the steel door ratchets open.

"Good God, you are one hard lady to find." A voice grumbles.

Dressed in combat-style pants and shirt, with his face painted black, Jacob Benson never looked better. I didn't think I'd be leaving this place alive. If I had time to cry manly tears over this, I might.

"About damn time, Benson."

His eyebrows raise in surprise at the body, but says nothing as he helps Esme to her feet, then offers me the same assistance. I grudgingly accept his help.

Benson checks his watch. "We've got approximately three minutes to evacuate the building before we get blown to pieces with the Torminas. What's the fastest exit, Jepsen?"

I force my mind past the fog of pain to remember the blueprints of the manor.

"We can leave through the service access. Head through the courtyard and out to the Amstel."

"Let's go."

Taking point, I adjust my stride to accommodate my injuries, picking up speed as we sprint through the main corridor of the basement then bolt up a stairway. At the top is the service exit with dark tinted glass.

Praying I won't have to smash a window, I quickly check behind for Benson and Esme. I hear them. Light-footed for Esme, heavy boots for Benson. Our combined breathing is a cacophony in the tomb-like corridors. We burst from the service exit into the courtyard and head for the Amstel. I slow my pace to gather Esme into my arms, then kick into survival. Legs burning, lungs protesting, we take long strides toward the inky black of the river as the world explodes at our backs.

We're thrown so hard I fall face first into the lip of the bank, losing Esme, and my breath. I search for her in the dark Amstel.

"Dayton!"

A second blast and the Tormina manor is pulverized. Flames lick the face of marble, roaring as it consumes whatever is in its path. Orange light billows outward producing a storm of embers. Fiery pillars of smoke rise higher. Some white hot debris lands close to the river. I flinch when a hand grasps mine and draws me from the vision.

"Dayton, we have to leave."

Eyes bleary, ears buzzing, I glance back and see Benson standing knee deep in the Amstel, one hand at his ear. Esme is beside me, our fingers laced. We're alive. My legs give out and I land in the muddy shallows.

"You're safe now, Esme."

"You are too. But we won't be for long if we stay here. The fire is coming this way."

"Esme, I think you should kiss me now."

She gives me a half-hysterical laugh, then presses her lips to mine in a desperate mating of mouths. I sigh, gripping her hair to keep her from breaking our connection, and even though I can hear the fire like a dragon belching over its meal, I cling tighter to her. Kiss her deeper until I'm as lightheaded as I want her to be.

"Never ever do this to me again, Dayton. And you must kiss me like you just did, every day. Every damn day."

"Every day?" I ask, smoothing strands of wet hair from her face, keeping her locked to my side, though I'm not yet standing. The adrenaline has faded and I'm weak.

"Damn, Skippy."

I laugh, wincing from the broken ribs, the bruises and wounds, and that blasted missing toe.

"I'm going to really enjoy being married to you."

"What?"

Capturing her surprised mouth with another kiss, I ignore Benson's *ahem* and lay my forehead against hers.

"I'm going to marry you. I would ask you, but you don't have a choice on the matter."

"Oh."

"I'm glad you aren't too broken up about it."

She grins, lashing one arm around my waist as we

groan to a stand. Benson falls into line beside me and gets the other side. Wading deeper into the Amstel, I smile at the dark abyss ahead of us.

"By the way, I wasn't going to give you a say on the matter either, so . . . there."

I raise a brow at Esme, who is chugging along, supporting half my weight in a sooty red ball gown. I couldn't have found a better woman.

"Oh?"

She nods sharply. "Benson, did you hear that? I'm going to marry Jepsen."

"Never saw it coming."

Charmed, exhausted, and ready to pass out, I laugh. "Try not to contain your enthusiasm. Just get us back to the getaway vehicle before you have to drag my ass."

Epilogue

Dayton

I've gone over it a hundred times. No, a thousand. And I can't remember how it all exactly happened.

Gazing out the expansive windows of the beach house hardly seems real. Not when I can see my wife of three months swishing ankle-deep in the surf, like some supermodel on the cover of Sports Illustrated.

She's lovely—will be even lovelier seven months from now.

Five months ago, I had been alone on this island. The Dominican Republic felt empty and secluded from the world. And I was a nest of indecision with no direction.

I laugh as Esme catches me spying and gestures for me to join her. It isn't a difficult decision.

I leave the remnants of our supper, go out to the pool, shimmering beneath the Caribbean sun. God, I missed home.

And that's what it is—no longer a place meant to give me respite from a reality I didn't want. But a place where I will raise my children and share my life.

"Brushing up on your sneaking skills, my love?"

I put my arms around Esme as we face the waves on our beach. Hell, it even sounds good. Three months and I feel like a kid on Christmas morning. Did I really marry this woman? Does she really love me the way I ache with it for her?

If I doubted it, the evidence growing beneath her flowing top is enough to convince me miracles do happen. She's carrying a little piece of both of us. And I've swung between terrified to recklessly proud in the last three months. Now, I want only to make Esme and our child happy and safe.

I nuzzle into her neck and inhale the fragrance of tanning oil and coconut. "I'm always ready for any opportunity."

"The heart of a Phantom . . . have you decided then?"

I rest my chin atop Esme's head and sigh. "Yes, I think I have."

"We'll have to split our time between here and Madrid."

"I know."

We remain silent with only the sound of rough water. I turn Esme so I can look her in the eye.

"You'd tell me if this was something you didn't want?"

"Of course. Dayton, I know how much you want to live our days on the island, with no outside contact. But you and I know we can't do that. You would grow restless. And so would I. I miss working. I miss the modeling business."

"Have you contacted them? Explained everything?"

"I didn't see how I could give them a good enough reason for leaving for two months without telling them why. And the why . . . well, does killing a man count as a good enough reason for a leave of absence?"

"I suppose that isn't a good idea then."

"No, but it's okay, because I've got some ideas." Her hands drop to her stomach, hardly showing, and she grins at me. "I think I might be starting my own business.

And I'm thinking Adrienne to be a pretty interested partner."

I rub my hands on her bare arms. I am so proud of her. "Zach will be thrilled. With my staying on as a trainer for the Phantoms and you giving him a grandchild, I think we'll be set for life on brownie points."

"My guess is, he'll be begging for more grandkids in a few years. I doubt the man will be happy with only one."

I chuckle, smoothing her hair, bringing her mouth closer as I whisper a kiss over her lips.

"There's an easy solution, you know."

"Mmmm," she answers, arms linking around my neck. "You do need practice to . . . you know."

Her breath rushes out when I dance several kisses down her neck. "Always be prepared."

"Yes." I dip to lift her into my arms, ignoring her protest. "I need lots . . . lots more practice for that."

The End.

Acknowledgements

Thank you to my amazing editor, Sharon Walling. Without her, I would be lost. She made this book possible and will likely be the reason I manage to get anything else published after. Thank you so, so much.

For more information about the author and the second book to the exciting Phantom Series, please visit the author's website at:

http://fillysaltz.wixsite.com/author

35808556R00123

Made in the USA
Middletown, DE
13 February 2019